'[*The Inheritors*] has everything we love about [Hannelore Cayre]; damaged but memorable characters, sharp language, ferocious humour, an undercurrent of political rage, a punchy narrative and lashings of subversion.' —*Lire*

'As corrosive as ever, the author of *The Godmother* unleashes her caustic eloquence in a hilariously black tale that mocks the self-perpetuation of the élite.' —*Paris Match*

'Social justice fuels the noir works of this author and lawyer: the little guys win, the powerful lose. So it was in *The Godmother*, in 2017, and so it is again, now more than ever, in *The Inheritors*.' —*Le Monde*

'[Cayre's] language takes your breath away, as the author so often does with her rapid-fire style.' —*Causette*

'A work of noir fiction worth its weight in gold.' —*Le Journal de Montréal*

'The author has a knack for producing one irresistibly eccentric character after another.' —*Les Echos Week-end*

'A funny, irreverent and exhilarating novel, in the purest tradition of French anarchistic crime novels.' —*Femme Actuelle Senior*

'A fabulous work of crime fiction – very funny and very politically incorrect – masterfully drawn by a specialist in the genre.' —Bernard Poirette, *Europe 1* podcast

HANNELORE CAYRE is a French writer, director and criminal lawyer. Her most recent work, *The Godmother*, won the European Crime Fiction Prize and the Grand Prix de Littérature Policière and has been shortlisted for a Crime Writers' Association Dagger award. *The Godmother* was also featured on *The New York Times*' '100 Notable Books of 2019' list and has been made into a major film starring Isabelle Huppert.

STEPHANIE SMEE left a career in law to work as a literary translator. Recent publications include the translations of Hannelore Cayre's *The Godmother*, and Françoise Frenkel's rediscovered World War II memoir *No Place to Lay One's Head*, which was awarded the JQ–Wingate Prize. Her translation of Joseph Ponthus' prize-winning work, *On the Line*, is forthcoming.

Book club notes are available for *The Inheritors* from blackincbooks.com.au

THE
INHERITORS

Published by Black Inc.,
an imprint of Schwartz Books Pty Ltd
Level 1, 221 Drummond Street
Carlton VIC 3053, Australia
enquiries@blackincbooks.com
www.blackincbooks.com

9781760642662 (paperback)
9781743821527 (ebook)

A catalogue record for this
book is available from the
National Library of Australia

Cover design by Akiko Chan
Text design and typesetting by Akiko Chan
Cover image: Martinedoucet/iStock

THE
INHERITORS

HANNELORE CAYRE
TRANSLATED BY STEPHANIE SMEE

It was in the moonless countryside, pitch black,
that I saw it for the first time, the green fluorescent rabbit,
vivid green in its abandoned field, living its life, oblivious
to its own peculiarity, in a burning halo, like when you
close your eyes to somebody's memory, a signal in the
black night, a small dot.

Olivier Cadiot, *Retour définitif et durable de l'être aimé*
(Definitive and Lasting Return of the Loved One)

'DO YOU THINK IT'S APPROPRIATE for a funeral, that outfit?'

'Yeah, I do, why? It's my nicest tracksuit ... The velour one! And anyway, have you looked in the mirror? You'd think ... But really, who gives a shit?'

She was right about that, Hildegarde, who gave a shit. It's true, we both looked like two spaced-out losers, and anyway, we'd be getting weird looks from everybody no matter what we decided to wear.

There was Juliette, my daughter, in khaki greens. She was going through her camo stage. And Pistachio and Geranium, our two ugly mutts wearing neither leash nor collar but sporting bows around their necks. Hildegarde, wearing her black velour tracksuit in an attempt to be chichi, and her size 46 black Nikes which she must have quickly dusted over with a rag. And then there was me, with my new Japanese titanium orthoses, which meant I could manage without my crutches. They pretty much had me goose-stepping when I walked, but it was improving every day. It's fair to say we stood out somewhat at the Trocadéro cemetery, where the de Rignys had their vault – smack-bang between the Dassault and Bouygues families.

1

A lot of people had come, seeing as I had made a statement by taking out the most expensive notice in *Le Figaro* to announce Tata's death, but none of them had acknowledged us. Worse still, a gap had emerged, a sort of *cordon sanitaire* between the three of us and everyone else which meant they could avoid being contaminated by our presence.

Who were they? Friends from bridge? People who filled their days going from one society event to another? Geriatrics who'd come to celebrate one of their idols taking such a long time to die? No idea! Eight months we had looked after Aunt Yvonne and we'd never received a single visitor at her townhouse mansion apart from her lawyer and her bank manager. All of this aside, though, I'm sure we were the ones most affected by her passing. The fact is we had grown attached to the old woman, especially when towards the end she was going so loopy she used to sing us Colette Renard's *Evenings of a Demoiselle*, inexplicably, all day long:

> *There'll be some sucking of the sweet*
> *Some stroking of the fish*
> *There'll be some starching of the shirt*
> *And some nibbling on a treat*

Which, at the age of ninety-eight, you'll admit shows quite some panache.

Be that as it may, she had now been dead for four days and I had become rich. Unimaginably rich. And because the rich are always in a hurry, I had more important things to do than hang around a cemetery. Our plane was leaving in six hours for our new home in the tax haven that is the British Virgin Islands – and the following Monday, because Monday's always a good day to start bringing about the end of the world, we would get to work.

Standing outside that vault, which the gravediggers no longer even bothered to seal given that the de Rignys were falling like flies (I'm not kidding, six in less than a year), I thought about our common forebear, Auguste. Whether his life story as I recount it in these pages reflects the life he truly lived, and whether his character was as I describe it is really neither here nor there.

Setting down those few months in the life of that appealing, yet slightly clueless young man is a way of rendering him flesh and blood, of giving him the immortality he deserves as a thank you for his gesture to my family. A way of extracting him from 'the dark backward and abysm of time', as Shakespeare would say. This way he'll find himself in the company of some other faithful fellows who may not exist in real life, but rather appear in those nineteenth-century novels that fashioned my political thinking and made me who I am.

Auguste had been sitting on the edge of his bed for more than an hour, eyes fixed on this costly novelty item available in the department stores, this thing called an *alarm clock*, which his aunt Clothilde had given him for his twentieth birthday.

Because we all know there will never be enough roosters in Paris to rouse you from your sleep, she had quipped in the note on the little card attached to the parcel.

It consisted of a clock which had been mounted inside a finely worked case portraying birds of paradise. Pondering the invention, the young man thought sadly how it would in many respects wreak havoc with the habits of all those night owls who, like him, struggled to rise in the morning. The thing was designed to set off a bell at a particular predetermined moment. In addition to the hands indicating hours and minutes, a special hand, which one would set the previous evening, marked the time to rise. Auguste had set that hand at the number seven, one hour prior to the time indicated on his summons to attend the draw.

This much-anticipated date had been haunting him since the month of October, when he had presented himself at the town hall for the census of the class of 1869, the year of his twentieth birthday. Trying not to dwell on the matter during the festive season, he had remained in a permanent state of inebriation until January, then had surprised himself by coming to see the draw as offering a conclusion to his agonising.

The countdown was finally over and today was the day!

This morning he would finally know if he drew a bad number, forcing him to abandon the Sorbonne – to give up his Parisian life, his pleasures, his indolent habits – for nine years of degrading military service, five of which would find him surrounded by brutish louts in damp barracks furnished with poor bedding.

The ring of that devilish invention made him jump, causing his innards to contract: *those not appearing for roll call at eight o'clock sharp shall be the first to be given their marching orders* were the words written at the foot of his call-up notice.

How he would have loved his mother and sister to accompany him to the draw. Unfortunately they had both been called as a matter of urgency to the bedside of an aunt who had taken ill. Nor was his father able to join him, confined to the house as he was with a poor back. That left his brother-in-law, Jules, a former officer turned businessman, and his brother, Ferdinand, an ambitious type who practised a cult-like devotion to money and whose favourite pastime was to back Auguste into a corner until he was ready to explode. Even if those two had offered to provide him with some comfort in the face of his ordeal, Auguste would have categorically refused.

The women of the family had not, however, abandoned him entirely, since they had arranged to have a mass said at Saint-Germain-de-Paris asking Providence to spare him the fate of military service. Obviously, Auguste did not believe in God: even less so since reading *On the Origin of Species*, a luminous beacon of a book that succeeded in scientifically refuting the grotesque notion of life as divine creation, but privately he told himself that neither could the prayers bought by his mother do him any harm.

He dressed hastily and made his way through the silent house, taking care not to wake anybody. Once over the threshold, he pulled his collar up to his ears, ready to launch himself into the inky darkness of that winter morning. But scarcely had he passed through the metal gate of his family home when his imagination bolted. He already pictured himself, fear in his belly, marching into battle, just as that ill-bred old soldier his parents insisted on inviting to dine at their table used to describe in words fit to terrify the ladies – a man by the name of Pélissier, a veteran of the dreadful siege of Sebastopol. In the halo of light cast by the gas street-lamps he could practically make out the twisted frozen corpses of horses half-eaten by soldiers.

As he made his way up Rue de la République, the dawn filled with the silhouettes of people whose snowy footprints were converging on the town hall of Saint-Germain-en-Laye. Children were playing battle games out the front of the building, entertaining the soldiers standing guard. Sitting astride imaginary mounts and armed with snowballs and sticks by way of swords, they launched themselves, shouting, at invisible enemies. Prussians, they said.

Those accompanying the young men were asked to remain outside while all those who had been called up were led by privates into the Hall of Honour. Sitting at the table waiting for them, with the municipal register containing the names of all the young men born in 1849 open in front of him, was the mayor, wearing his sash of red, white and blue, together with an impatient officer flanked by a handful of soldiers.

Auguste went to join a small group of bourgeois civilians standing around a large coal brazier, who had been joined, naturally enough, by the offspring of their servants. He greeted the Bertelot boy, who he knew had harboured designs on his cousin at some point, as well as his childhood friend Duchaussois, whom his father was constantly holding up as an example after he had pursued a position in the magistracy. He saw his high-school friends Berquet, Bruault and Fromoisin ... and there was Portefaux, too, the son of the mortgage registrar. Auguste hardly recognised him he had gained so much weight: he was hoping to be declared unfit for service on the grounds of obesity, he said. Auguste was equally surprised to see the fellow whom his mother had always called *little Perret*, the youngest son of their gardener, who it seemed had been born the same year as him. Then there were the sons of the town's shopkeepers. Some of them he knew from church, from having played with them when he was younger, or simply from having glimpsed them at the back of their parents' shops. A cheerful hubbub was very quickly heard emerging from this inner circle.

A little removed, keeping a respectful distance from the stove, stood a crowd of young workers clad in factory coats, as well as a few peasants battling silently against the cold, dressed as if heading to Mass. They had all made the effort to put on clean clothes, for if their poverty was tolerated it was only because they had made the effort to dress properly and did not allow their impoverishment to cause offence to those with whom they were required to rub shoulders.

Auguste could not help but observe them surreptitiously.

'There are so many of them,' he thought, astonished. 'How awkwardly they conduct themselves, and how stubborn their silence. Their manner sits at such odds with the ease and civility of the well-to-do. Why are they not the ones approaching the stove so they might warm their bones, with their meagre clothes and inadequate shoes, so poorly suited to the cold?'

'These poor lads had a price, it seems. How much for that sturdy specimen hopping from one clog to another so as not to freeze? And would he agree to sell himself, that man, if he weren't given his marching orders? Did *he* think that to have himself killed in the place of the son of a wealthier family is "a matter of outlook" as Monsieur Thiers recently asserted in the Chamber? Did he think it self-evident, a given, much like conceding his place around the fire?'

'How complicated it all is!' he thought, sighing.

Despite the Emperor's desire to bring some ethics to the trade in men, the principle of freedom to contract had once again triumphed in the Chamber as a result of pressure exerted by the country's paterfamilias.

The liberal deputies had voted by overwhelming majority in favour of bringing back military substitution as it had been practised prior to the accession of Napoléon III. Thus, it was no longer a question of the state being responsible for finding a replacement, in exchange for a fee, for those young men refusing to go, but rather a matter for the families themselves. There had of course been the minor socialist group led by Jules Simon protesting this *white slave trade*, this resurgence of *traffickers in human flesh* – but it was against a backdrop of general indifference. The conservatives, for their part, had brandished the spectre of war with Prussia. And contrary to all expectations, that country, while considerably smaller than France, had just crushed Austria at Sadowa in a single battle, thanks entirely to its compulsory service and its army of 1,200,000 men, but the conservatives too had been preaching in the wilderness.

At around ten o'clock, the officer present started to call the roll that had been stripped of exemptions, while a soldier turned the handle of the drum containing the 127 numbers slotted into their wooden casings.

Each time a name was called to be drawn, Auguste, who was not only in a state of panic but also bad at mathematics, would jump and lose track of his reasoning: 'There are 167 on the list, and twenty of them are exempted, so given that the municipality has to supply twenty-five men and assuming there'll be ten discharged for various reasons, a number would become truly bad from twice that, so from fifty, which means there's one chance in …'

Duchaussois was the first of the little group around the

coal stove to be called. Were he to draw an unlucky number, he would seek to rely on a document he had thought to have prepared by a public prosecutor of the Imperial Court in Paris who was a family friend, which referenced his position as an acting judge on the Seine Tribunal, a position he had occupied for three years without remuneration. He drew a 10, asserted his claim, and was exempted.

Portefaux was the next name to be called ...

After hesitating for some minutes as he mumbled who knows what sort of incantation, the young man was called to order and pushed unceremoniously towards the urn for the draw. When he extracted the number from its casing, he started to weep with relief: 120.

'You'll be able to start your diet, you great lazy oaf,' mocked the soldier, as he returned to cranking the handle of the drum.

At last, around midday, it was Auguste's turn.

When his name was called, his face crumpled. His body felt like it weighed a tonne as he dragged himself to the urn, plunged in his hand, then yanked it out as if from boiling water.

'A 4,' he murmured, defeated.

'Selected!' cried the officer, before reeling off the relevant articles of the Code in an emotionless voice. 'Monsieur, in view of your number and unless you qualify for discharge, your position in the contingent is hereby confirmed. The recruitment board shall make its announcement on 18 July, whereupon you may proffer such replacement as you may have identified from any *département* in the Empire. The mayor shall inform you of the conditions of said replacement's acceptance, as well as any documents you may be called upon to produce. We are relying on your zeal in performing your duty, and remind you of the unfortunate consequences which shall befall both you and your family in the event of your failure to comply.'

Auguste remained frozen before the soldier, his eyes vacant, hands moist, mind adrift. Then another name was called and he was forced to move, shoved aside by the next person to draw. He left the town hall without acknowledging a soul; in any event, nobody would have welcomed his greetings, for now he was jinxed. Overcome, he headed home, where his father was waiting impatiently to know what action to take.

Despite his outwardly calm and confident demeanour, Casimir had always worried for his youngest son.

Once the boy had passed his baccalaureate, he had done his best to initiate him into the delights of public construction – there was no memory of any de Rigny having ever done anything else, at least since Colbert – but so vacant were Auguste's eyes on the occasion of his last site visit that Casimir had sadly concluded the boy was not at all suited to such matters. This was in stark contrast to his other son. Ferdinand, having adopted and made his own the extraordinary legal construct that was the public limited company – namely an ability to conduct business without any liability for its failures – had managed the remarkable feat of quadrupling his assets by the age of twenty-seven, while taking like a duck to the troubled waters of awarding public contracts.

'What's to become of this boy and his unhealthy sensitivity?' Casimir would often wonder if he happened to be pondering his son Auguste. 'He seems incapable of imagining doing anything with himself.'

He saw only one explanation for the significant difference between his two children: whereas the eldest, Ferdinand, had developed both in strength and energy, the youngest had succumbed in quick succession to every conceivable illness from the day he was born – and, like every child wrestled from death, he had been far too spoiled by his mother.

Physically he belonged to that species of tall, thin types with a broad forehead and dead-straight blond locks that he flicked off his face. His large dark eyes shone like horse chestnuts, lending him a fanatical air, as if ravaged from within, with a slightly effeminate touch. He considered himself a philosopher or poet, or both, coming out with particularly infuriating inanities such as: 'I'd love to learn a manual trade so I might help my fellow man, brother to brother.' He would go around predicting that he would die at thirty-three, like Christ, which women found highly entertaining. His parents, much less so.

After turning family mealtimes into a great headache by declaring suddenly one day that he was adopting a Pythagorean diet, a regime spurning all animal flesh, his latest infatuation was socialism, or more precisely the writings of a philosopher – a certain Marx – who was living in exile in England, about whom he would harp on endlessly at every opportunity. This most recent fad had disrupted the household's peace and quiet once and for all, with the two brothers constantly bickering, each time further testing the limits of acceptability. It had reached the point where Casimir had had to beg his sister Clothilde, who lived in Paris, to take Auguste in so as to remove him from Saint-Germain until he had had a chance to mature.

Clothilde herself was not without her failings.

For starters, her lodgings were not at all appropriately located for a woman living on her own. Instead of settling in an area such as the 16th, 8th or 7th arrondissement of the capital, Clothilde had purchased an apartment for an exorbitant price in Haussmann's new developments in the heart of the Grands Boulevards, surrounded by cafés and theatres. To make matters worse, she meddled in politics. A committed Republican and devotee of a certain Léon Gambetta, a young arrogant lawyer with a visceral dislike of the Emperor, she would loiter in courtrooms and clubs so she could listen to his speeches. And to complete the picture, she was single – *I wish to remain a free woman and not be a poor turkey under the guardianship of some halfwit who has assumed control of her money* – so, lacking a husband with whom Casimir might reasonably have been able to discuss the possibility of reining her in, and at the age of fifty-six, it was obviously too late. Notwithstanding these few imperfections and the fact she set a deplorable example for the women of the family, she remained nonetheless socially acceptable. Unfortunately, the same could no longer be said of Auguste, who in addition to having transformed his home into a battlefield had managed to set himself in out-and-out opposition to his social peers.

An optimist by nature, Casimir had gambled on his sister's modernity to guide his young son gently towards a more moderate stance. What's more, they would each be looking out for the other, which could hardly hurt.

When Auguste appeared in the dining room looking all undone, dinner had already been served and the three men of the family – his father, his brother-in-law Jules and his older brother Ferdinand – were waiting for him before beginning.

'Well then?' asked Casimir, anxiously.

'Judging by the look on his face, I'd say he's drawn a bad number!' said Ferdinand in a mocking voice.

'You'll be pleased. I drew a 4,' replied Auguste with a sigh, before collapsing onto his chair.

His father reassured him.

'You mustn't worry for a moment, I had made provision, as I did for your brother, and had set aside the 2000 francs required by the state to pay for your exemption. But given this damnable law, and the fact we now have to go about finding you a replacement ourselves, I'll have ample means to pay a dealer to bring us a good one. I've already approached Kahn & Levy at Place Saint-Opportune, who reportedly have no shortage of men.'

'Was it in that rag published by your friend Tripier that you found your Jewish dealers in human flesh listed?' asked Auguste's brother-in-law, Jules.

'Between an advertisement for the *Naudia measuring stick* and *Learning German made simple!*' said Ferdinand, not to be outdone.

'The *Assurance* is not a rag but a newspaper for decent family men. The recruiting board will convene on 18 July, which leaves us, all of us – and let me insist on this point, *all of us* – six short months to find a replacement for our dear Auguste.'

Casimir himself still harboured very unpleasant memories from the period that had preceded the ballot of his own class. He had been left in a state of uncertainty right up to the eleventh hour, after a quarrel with his mother led her to punish him by steadfastly refusing to pay for a replacement for him in the event he drew a bad number. It still made him anxious to remember the day, twenty-three years earlier, when, in that same town hall, he had plunged a trembling hand into the urn. Fortunately, fate had smiled upon him and he had drawn a good number. He would not have to head off. And the events of 1848 only served to underline his relief. 'I felt the wind of the cannonball in my hair,' he was wont to recall. So there was no question of having his sons suffer that same dreadful experience, especially Auguste, who, given his feeble constitution, would struggle more than most with life in the barracks.

'With the Prussians bearing down on us like a locomotive, I suspect prices will climb and your measly 2000 francs will do little to attract the dealers as you would hope. Believe you me, we shall have our work cut out,' pointed out brother-in-law Jules, who knew a thing or two about conscription, having squandered a third of his existence wallowing in the dreary routine of garrison life.

'There's no doubt that with the rumours of war, those hustlers are set to earn more buying and selling men than trading livestock,' agreed Ferdinand, his mouth full.

Despite feeling everybody's eyes focused upon him, Auguste stared at his plate as if into an abyss. His father placed a reassuring hand on his forearm and said, gently:

'Do you think we're not mindful of what's troubling you? Military replacements are a good thing precisely because they help to restore the very social equity of which you're so fond. It causes money to fall from the hands of those who have it into the empty hands of those who have none, to ensure, at the end of the day, that the army is supplied with a good soldier rather than a poor-quality one. Don't listen to the foolish notions planted in your head by those socialists whose company you keep. By removing them from the foul air of their workplace, and by relieving them of their bad food, military service offers nothing but benefits to the proletariat, whereas it serves only to compromise the health of the sons of the bourgeoisie and ruin their careers. This inequality you're constantly talking to us about is found precisely in the absurd notion of universal service.'

Ferdinand intervened.

'There is a much easier way to explain all of this to my dear brother: any proletarian worker with a true job will never be used as a replacement. It's only ever an issue for a labourer who has no work and who, by definition, constitutes a menace. There's no need to delve any further into the whys or wherefores: it's a simple matter of rounding up the riff-raff and confining them to the garrisons in order to stave off chaos! Isn't that right ... Auguste ...'

And conscious of his son's despondency, Casimir finished on a gentle note, as if conversing with an invalid:

'Tell yourself it's *time* we're buying, not a man ...'

'Time to refine your grand leftist theories, which one day are sure to benefit society,' came Ferdinand's merciless mockery, prompting mad laughter from brother-in-law Jules, who, desperately struggling to contain himself, narrowly avoided spitting his soup onto the tablecloth.

'In the barracks, they'll begrudge Auguste his education and scorn him for his qualities!' said his father, losing his temper.

'His qualities? What qualities?' said his brother, pretending to call for a response from around the table.

And then suddenly, as if struck by lightning, Casimir started:

'But of course!' he cried. 'How did I not think of it sooner? Why not ask the young Perret lad to replace you? It may well be that he drew a favourable number. And to think we're preparing to send people off on a hunt to the other side of the country when the solution may well be here, right under our very noses! Adèle ... Adèle ...'

He beat the floor with his walking stick as he shouted for the maid:

'Adèle! Adèle, in the name of God!'

'Yes, Monsieur ...'

'Adèle, where's the gardener?'

Auguste, who until then had remained silent, suddenly struck the table with his fist, causing everyone present to jump.

'That's enough. It's abominable! Perret's boy will not be sent in my place! I will never agree to it! His poor family will not pay that bloody impost when we have the means to buy ourselves out of it for the cost of an annual subscription to a box at the Opera.'

'Aaaaaaaah, here we go!' groaned his brother.

And calling the other two as his witnesses, he said:

'The moment has finally arrived when he gets to lecture us on the topic of human misery!'

Then, grabbing the ladle to fill Auguste's plate to over-flowing, Ferdinand said:

'Here, have a little more of this excellent soup so you can take your time telling us about all these poor people, because after all there's nothing better than a handsome table bedecked with flowers and silverware to bring out socialist sentiments. Come on, get on with it, we're all ears! Tell us, for example, about your friends from the Café du Madrid ... Or – now what is he called again? That shame-ful Jew who seems to have scribbled some sort of treatise on the right to steal? – Marx, is that it? Go on, tell us a bit about your Monsieur Marx!'

Infuriated, Auguste left the table immediately, fists clenched, his mouth full of all the abominable insults he would so dearly have loved to spit in his brother's face, but he contained himself out of respect for his father, who he felt had already put up with enough for one day.

He could still hear his brother shouting as he fled to his room.

'—And you just sit there without saying a word. "I love the people," he cries, the fool … Instead of letting him get away with everything and leaving him in the care of that lunatic Aunt Clothilde, you should be putting your foot down! Because when he gets it into his head to go and enlighten the hoi polloi about the principles of Goodness, Truth and Beauty, and he's brought back to you in pieces from Paris on some oxcart, everybody here will be weeping – everybody except me! And anyway, I've had enough of eating this peasant's food when Monsieur does us the honour of turning up!'

And with that, Ferdinand set the cutlery dancing across the cloth and left the table.

Jules observed his plate somewhat sceptically.

'It's true that without any bacon this soup is not very tasty!'

Hastily gathering together the few things he had brought with him, the young man hurried out of the house so as not to miss the train that would take him back to Paris. But arriving at the station and seeing the crowds gathered at the roundhouse, he realised many people had taken advantage of the sunny weather to head out to the snowy countryside. As a result, he was unlikely to find a seat in first class for his return journey, nor even one in second. That left third, even though he did not have enough layers to join the clerks and workers in the open carriage.

There, gathered in that railway station – built, not without irony, by Casimir de Rigny himself – was a microcosm of French society. A woman in clogs, burdened with a brood of grubby children, was rubbing shoulders with a *grande dame* flanked by her maid and doll-like offspring, all heading home from an outing. A respectable husband from Saint-Germain-en-Laye, off to the capital to breach the conjugal monotony, offered his seat to a young dancer from the Opéra Comique who was on her way back to her aged patron. A host of aspiring millionaires and young artists, loaded up with masterpieces, crossed paths at the station with their down-at-heel counterparts heading home and cursing Paris. There were thieves about too, one eye on that handbag somebody had forgotten to watch, the other on a wallet poking out.

All these social theatrics were a world away from Auguste's preoccupations; in his mind, he was already dead, absurdly alone, his body impaled on a Prussian bayonet in the middle of a field.

No sooner had the carriage doors opened than the compartments were stormed. The young man, having purchased his ticket at the last minute, ended up in the third-class carriage, precisely as he had anticipated. He began his journey jammed between two stocky workers stinking of sweat, who were greatly amused by their proximity to this young, sweet-scented chap. Upon arrival in Pecq, people took pity on him, seeing as he was blue with cold, and he was shoved into the second-class carriage. There he was able to warm himself up, drowning in a gaggle of young women being scolded by their mothers. They were returning from an arranged rendezvous with attractive potential Saint-Germain-en-Laye suitors, but despite the photographs sent in advance, the train tickets, the money spent on outfits and ribbons, no understanding had been reached. 'No, truly, you simply make no effort at all!' railed their mothers. The young ladies were not listening, content to giggle as they pretended not to eye Auguste all the way back to Gare Saint-Lazare.

1

FROM THE MINUTE I BOARDED the TGV, I had the shits with everything.

I don't like having people in my space, so I never sit in my allocated seat. I can't stand my legs touching my neighbour's, not to mention having to do battle over the armrest. I prefer the flip seats near the doors, even if you rarely get any peace there because the space is often crammed with idiots letting rip or old people who, having just got on, are busy phoning to say they're on their way – *I can't hear you anymore, can you hear me? Hello?*

That day it was four girls who looked like they'd stepped straight out of a rap video, taking selfies from every possible angle. Curious, I checked out #TGVParis-Brest on Instagram to see how they'd glorified themselves, and to see what attributes they'd unveiled to the grand twenty-first-century fairground of seduction. But there, amid those images of curvy booty and pouting, swollen lips ready for every sort of stimulation imaginable, somebody – without my realising – had taken a photo of me looking on, and posted it.

There I was, in my black mini dress with pockets, my bomber jacket, my legs fitted out with their orthoses and my little heeled ankle boots, lost in a cloud of rainbow-coloured parrots. The total casting error. Emily the Strange invited to the hos' birthday party.

And to top it all off, I was pulling one of those faces ...

I've got to say, I wasn't feeling at the top of my game. I'd just been put on compulsory sick leave because I'd narrowly avoided being sliced in two, width-wise, by the doors of a metro train and, to make matters worse, I was on my way to the ultimate bore of a destination, namely my father's eighty-fifth birthday.

And the trip was a long way from over: once I'd made it to Brest, I would still have an hour by bus and an hour and a half by boat over wild seas to go. And since I knew that as soon as I arrived I'd just be in the way, you can imagine my enthusiasm.

I knew the script by heart: once I was there, my father would pretend to be happy to see me, then, after the customary banalities – *Did you eat anything on the train? Were there a lot of people on the boat? When are you leaving again?* – he'd have nothing more to say to me. I'd be all, *And you? How are things with you?* knowing all the while that I'd be opening the floodgate to a litany of grievances. Granny Soize calls it *the kaleidoscopic whinge*: sentences which, when taken in isolation and uttered in a neutral tone, sound purely informative – *You know, I was at the doctor... When I eat in the morning, I get vertigo ... You remember Dédé, they're going to cut off his hands and feet because of his diabetes* – and yet when they're all gathered together produce a terrifying pattern of the fate about to befall him. He swivels it a bit, and wham! everything gets rearranged and off we go again. The most awful thing is, it never stops.

It was raining at Brest, just for a change. A biblical horizontal rain driven by the wind from the open sea that whips you in the face as soon as you step off the train. It was then that I noticed them for the first time, the three Parisians, there on the platform. It must be said they were the only thing you noticed, standing there in their pretty little shower-proof raincoats in an attempt to ward off the torrents of water. Two hirsute hipsters, one of whom was wearing glasses, as well as a fairly plain, tall girl with long, glossy hair.

I limped to the bus station as quickly as I could and climbed into the bus, which stank of wet dog. And then every oldie on board fell all over me. *What a long time it's been! You're as white as a baby's bottom, aren't you! And what about your daughter, where is she? Blah, blah, blah* ... Fortunately, in this part of the world, it's only one kiss you cop, not four, because I had to make my way down the whole aisle. The door shutting in the faces of the three dripping Parisians was met with general indifference, seeing as the bus was intended primarily for those from the island who were heading home.

Once we arrived at the port, everybody got off in a single movement and rushed to the ferry terminal to wait out of the rain until we were able to embark.

My old friend Tiphaine was there, sitting on a bench, busy yelling at her children to stop mucking about with the coffee dispenser. It was only when I saw how tall her youngest was that I realised it had been eons since I'd been back to see my father. All I remembered was a little infant where now there was a little girl with curls piled on top of her head standing firmly on her own two feet and staring at me as I interposed myself between her and her mother.

I kissed my friend, embracing her generous, full body in a hug, and was struck with a flash of realisation that I had been missing my island.

Generally speaking, when you see old friends after a long separation, you tend to feel a little uncomfortable, as if prisoner of a bond that isn't always easy to reignite, but that's never the case with people from around here. I think it's because our families have been split in two for centuries, the men at sea either in the Navy or the Merchant Marine, and the women left behind ashore looking after the children. Living on the island then meant we developed a special gift for communicating with those who were absent.

So, after merely wondering where I had left off in the great ongoing drama that was the island ... Was it before they rebuilt the cemetery wall or after the Spar supermarket had closed down? ... she just said, 'Oh, right, yeah. It really is quite a while since you've been back!'

The weight of time that had passed since my previous visit required Tiphaine to address the basics: who had died, who was having an affair with whom, who had drowned, who had been evacuated by helicopter – so many tragedies for such a small place – she might have been accused of over-egging the number of dramatic incidents, but no. It really is like that around here; terrible stuff happens all the time!

We all made our way on board in the pouring rain, including the three tourists, who arrived by taxi in a state of chaos.

I headed straight for the bow of the boat and stretched out on a row of four seats, eyes closed, head resting on a sweater. Yes, I get seasick. I've tried everything: pharmaceuticals, hypnosis, simulator, even the thing where you take a nap under an apple tree; all of which is to say, I have fought it, but my body, not content with being a fractious, recalcitrant hack, has assigned me to shore duty.

The Parisians were sitting a few metres away from where I had lain down and, as I had nothing else to do on the crossing but listen to them, I allowed myself to be soothed by their conversation.

I worked out that they were a couple who had brought along their friend, the bespectacled hipster, in an attempt to take his mind off things. The tall, plain girl had concocted an itinerary, which she spelled out item by item, pointing out the places to visit on a map of the island. Somebody had died: it seemed to have been the girlfriend of glasses-man, because he was talking angrily about the father of his late sweetheart – a conservative member of parliament whom he called *the Super Prick* – and about his attitude at the funeral. It seems he had used the ceremony as he would a garden party, making his way from group to group, flanked by a waiter who was handing out glasses of champagne, trying to extricate himself and his son from the morass of their legal difficulties. Then there was talk of an earthquake in Nepal. They mentioned towns I'd never heard of. While the couple, who appeared to be involved in humanitarian work, were talking about a sanitation disaster, the one who had lost his girlfriend bitterly quoted the law of deaths to kilometres: the further away the event, the more victims are required in order to stir the interest of a minimum number of people. Nobody had given a shit about the earthquake in Nepal with its hundreds of victims – his chick among them – crushed under tonnes of rocks.

For whatever reason, I fell asleep with two lines of Philippe Muray's 'Tomb for an Innocent Tourist' ringing in my head:

There's nothing so beautiful as a blonde tourist
Right before her head falls off in the jungle.

My father had sent his mate Fañch in his Renault 14 to fetch me from the boat. Fañch threw my bag into the back and hardly had I plonked myself down in the passenger seat before he started giving me grief.

'You know, he's old, your father, he won't be having too many more birthdays, you have to come more often, otherwise one day you'll regret it … And when you do come, stay for longer and bring your daughter with you …'

It's crazy the way this community tries to slip leg irons on you every time you come home, I thought to myself.

'He told you he was missing me, is that it?' I gave it right back to him. He grumbled something in reply, his florid drunkard's conk buried deep in the fur of his spaniel, who was perched between him and the steering wheel. And then he was silent.

It must be said that everybody has an opinion on what we shall call *the topic of Blanche* on this pebble of an island, where everybody feels responsible for everyone else's kids, if only because in that environment, shut off from the rest of the world, they all grow up right under your nose, so nobody is indifferent to *the topic of Blanche*.

There's one in every generation in a closed-off community, the one who's a pain in the neck. The sort of ratbag who's always involved in the latest scandal. Whenever a holiday house is broken into or a car set alight . . . Whenever lobsters disappear from the traps or the jetty walls are tagged in high season with filthy comments attacking tourists . . . To put it bluntly, for the generation of those born in the '80s, that historical pain in the arse was me: Blanche de Rigny.

There was the time I ran away, of course, when after yet another fight with my father he wanted to stick me in a boarding school on the mainland before I'd finished middle school. Three days of searching. National rescue helicopters circling the coastline of the island. Every vessel out in the water, right down to the smallest dinghy, carrying out a meticulous search for my body at the foot of the cliffs when, at age thirten, I had left to try to make a living on the streets of Paris. Already.

Better still, even before all of that, there was my birth.

It happened in the middle of a gale, like every other time there's a drama on this fucking island. My father was at sea off the coast of Africa when my mother started haemorrhaging, and seeing as it's impossible to fly a helicopter in a 50-knot wind, the lifeguards had to ferry her to the mainland by boat. Obviously I had not been born yet, but I've been told the story so many times I can see myself standing between the legs of the sailors' wives, watching the orange and green lifeboat that would take her to hospital slip down its rails and into the water. Not one of the guys from the national lifeguards hesitated, so the story goes; their wives were weeping because there were walls of water and they feared they'd never see their husbands alive again. During the crossing my mother bled out in front of the powerless men. She was dead on arrival, but me, seriously premmie at only six months, I survived. One of the lifeguards registered my birth at the Brest town hall, and, keen not to make a faux pas, gave me my mother's first name: Blanche. They also say that when, some days later, my father returned for the funeral, the lifeguards all went to greet him as he came off the boat, looking as devastated as if it were their fault. They were the ones who carried the coffin in their orange uniform. The church was so full the priest had to leave the front door open. The latest instalment in this drama on the high seas saw the island banding together around the widower, the father of the tiny little girl battling in an incubator all alone on the mainland.

Thinking back on it, perhaps that's the reason I get seasick.

After the funeral, Pater departed quick smart for one of his longest tours at sea, entrusting me to his aunt, Granny Soize, the woman who brought me up and who took care of my every need on a daily basis. He only took his retirement from the Merchant Marine super-grudgingly when all that remained for an old guy like him was the fitting out of rust-buckets filled with Filipinos.

I was twelve years old by the time he started living with us full-time and it goes without saying he was entirely unwelcome, his unsavoury machismo misfiring completely after his lifelong absence.

Every place prompts its own particular set of destinies, so prior to my escape I must have subconsciously sensed that I had to get the hell away from that island and its constant dramas at all costs before I suffered my own calamity, *in personam* ... And I wasn't wrong about that.

It's a pretty banal story when all's said and done, and as you'd expect, entirely typical of the island, for anybody in the know ... We were taking advantage of the fact that the police hadn't yet arrived for the summer season by indulging in one of our favourite pastimes as idle youth, namely taking one of the cars parked at the wharf for a joy-ride. The keys were always left hanging in the ignition, and we were hammered and had no licence. Here we go, guys! We're outta here ... I was with some guys and girls from the camping ground, not kids from the island, otherwise it would never have played out the way it did.

I was sitting in – or, rather, I was squashed into – the backseat, unfortunately too pissed to realise that the idiot who was driving was taking the coast road.

He simply didn't see that the earth stopped there. *Finis terrae.* Boom, over the cliff. The two guys in the front were crushed to death and the girl next to me burnt alive, because she had been sensible enough to put on her belt and got stuck. Seeing as I've never been sensible about anything, I flew through the rear window when the car rolled and broke my spine.

Paris
12 June 1870

Since drawing a bad number in the ballot, Auguste had spent some ghastly nights tortured by anxiety.

Ever since that cursed day, he had continued to set his alarm clock for 7 am, but having only ever snatched one or two hours' rest when it rang, he would switch it off and go back to sleep, managing only to drag himself from his bed in the late afternoon. He had not set foot in the university for two months on account of his constant headaches, and relations with his aunt Clothilde had deteriorated considerably.

Recently returned from viewing the new collection at the Printemps department store, his aunt was in splendid humour, but her mood soured irreparably upon coming into her salon to find her nephew, much like the previous day, and the day before that, prone on her sofa like a bundle of linen and moaning, a damp cloth wrapped around his head.

With a deep sigh, she let her displeasure be known.

'Oh please, Aunt, need you shout? My head is giving me such grief that I'm at the point of wondering if some creature has not been hiding in my pillow and feeding on my brain during the night.'

She swept away his words with an exasperated gesture.

'You have a letter from your father.'

'Oh, will you not read it to me ...' said Auguste, in a feeble voice. 'I can scarcely open my eyes.'

'I have had more than enough of your using my apartment as some sort of health spa where there's nothing to be done but sleep and have one's linen laundered. Read the letter yourself!' And she retrieved the envelope from the table and dropped it on his face.

Auguste waited until she had left the room before breaking its seal.

The news was not good.

The Jewish company on Place Sainte-Opportune that arranged military replacements, and which was supposedly bursting at the seams with men for sale, had proved a dead end: it had been plundered and had not a single man to offer, despite an advance payment of 1000 francs. In the end, Monsieur Levy had provided a refund, but the problem remained; agencies all across Paris were suffering similar shortages. So, they would have to make do without them. His father had then come up with the idea of sending a letter to all his suppliers enjoining them to enquire of innkeepers, coachmen, cobblers and priests – all those occupations who have constant dealings with others – in order to find out if they knew of any out-of-work labourers who would agree to sell themselves to the father of a well-to-do family. Unfortunately, nor had this course of action produced any result.

He had also written to a distant cousin down in the Basque country, but the law of primogeniture in that part of the world had had such a devastating effect that every available young man had left for America. Nor was there any joy to be had in agricultural regions such as Normandy, or the north of France, with the only available substitutes being acquired for outrageous sums by local landowners as replacements for their sons.

He was being advised he would do better to continue his search in the larger towns. One of his stone suppliers in Bordeaux had been a whisker away from locating him a replacement. The son of a water merchant, who had also drawn a bad number but who, by virtue of having a brother already in the service, had been exempted and was thus free to sign up. But just as the matter was about to be settled, a notary had snaffled the man up for the astronomical figure of 10,000 francs.

He was also being advised to consider returned servicemen, who were highly prized by recruitment boards for substitution purposes. His envoys in the Orne region had thus been on the lookout for such a rare gem and had ended up locating a young soldier who might well have taken Auguste's place: a man by the name of Roussel, who had been discharged with a leg wound but who had spent two years recuperating. He stood at five foot three, incisors and canines intact, and although he was quite unattractive and prone to haemorrhoids, his legs, so it was said, were once again beyond criticism. His price was to be negotiated by his uncle, with whom he lodged, but the latter would consider nothing less than 9000 francs, half of which was to be paid in advance, which Casimir considered too steep a price given the candidate's dubious constitution. However, the man very quickly found a taker and was acquired by the broker for a Parisian insurance company, who had come all the way to that part of the world to solicit business.

Every time they have been ready to settle, the distances involved have brought it all undone. I personally negotiated three deals at Laon, Orléans and Beauvais, none of which came through on account of the sort of people with whom I was dealing, and I have lost no less than 800 francs, what with the three journeys, the cost of lodgings, the advances paid, the brokers and the meals I was required to offer them.

One thing is now clear: there is not so much as a single man of five foot one to be had for thousands of leagues around for less than 8000 francs. But worry not. We shall extricate you from this cursed conscription and I am certain you shall soon have your sister's husband to thank, for he has taken the matter in hand. As a former soldier, he knows the taverns where these people drink and knows better than anyone how to talk to them. He proposed setting off for Toulon, where the African contingents land, but your sister has objected. It seems that town has become a cesspit where every dealer from the capital engaged in the trade of men is looking for stock. When a boat arrives, the insurance company agents and brokers appear, their pockets lined with gold, seeking to extract the signature of soldiers weakened by tropical fevers and infirmities after their long voyage at sea. They entice them into disreputable establishments, where they are drugged and encouraged to spend the substitution price they have not yet been paid on whores and orgies. The broker who has encouraged them to drink up then promises them 6000 francs and pays them only half that amount, the balance being set off against the cost of their debauchery, which is calculated at a usurious rate. He then sells them on

*for 10,000 francs to poor fathers who are willing to make any
sacrifice in order to save their boy. In any event, I read in
my friend Tripier's paper that the recruitment boards had
received very strict orders to refuse these damaged, cast-off
soldiers from Africa.*

*Your brother-in-law has thus settled upon Brittany,
where, it seems, he is owed some favours by old acquaintances. He has written to them. And now we're waiting.*

Auguste let out a plaintive sigh as he refolded his father's
letter, and then he stood up.

'Aunt, I'm heading out!'

No answer.

He encountered her outside at the entrance porch to the
building amid all the other residents of Rue du 10 Décembre, swooning before a troop of cuirassiers sitting proudly
astride their mounts. The reflection of spring sunshine off
armoured breastplates and the trembling of the ground
under the horses' hooves lent the atmosphere a warlike
frisson, galvanising onlookers to the point where they nigh
lost their voices bawling *To Berlin! To Berlin!*

Clothilde, who in the ordinary course would have pep-
pered him with questions the moment he set foot outside
the apartment, spared him not so much as a glance, so
preoccupied was she with gazing at the soldiers' tanned
faces under their helmets, their powerful muscles, their
puffed-up chests. Observing her surreptitiously, he noted
in horror that despite her fifty-six years, she was quivering
with desire as she inhaled the powerful smell of these battle-
ready creatures through flared nostrils.

'Aunt, I'm heading out!' he repeated deliberately, raising his voice.

'I'm making another attempt to invite the Gonthier-Joncourts and their daughter to my Tuesday salon. I've been meaning to speak to you about it. I expect you to be at your best.'

'Love is far too significant a matter simply to marry some eyesore in order to avoid military service. And anyway, in order to be exempted on the grounds of having to *support the family*, one must make the claim *prior* to the draw and not after the event! So, it is too late.'

'Had you listened to me —'

'Remind me, these people, they make bricks, do they not? Or are they in coal? Or is it patents? If I may be so bold, Aunt, you are ill-placed to speak to me of marriage – you, who have always been so opposed to it!'

'That has nothing to do with it, as you very well know. If women are still marrying, it is because they are unaware of the law. But *you*, you are not a woman. And yes, these people are in coal, but *you*, might I remind you, are in nothing. And the goose who is hoping one day for a fool to steal away her inheritance is Eulalie, her parents' only daughter – and I would have loved the fool in this story to be you.'

'At just nineteen years of age Mademoiselle Eulalie already has the proportions of a well-built country notary. Imagine how she will look at thirty! And anyway, she's a sweet girl who certainly deserves better than a man who shall never love her.'

His aunt shrugged her shoulders and exhaled.

'You will not be stealing that Gonthier-Joncourt girl

from anybody, and well she knows it. As do her parents. A match with a proper young lady, even an unpromising one, who offers you the means to pursue your passion for ... for philosophical reflection, would be of far greater use to you than those good-for-nothings loitering about in your socialist cafés. You want to devote your existence to pondering the universe? So be it. A de Rigny may do with his life whatsoever he wishes, but he is forbidden from being poor!'

Clothilde articulated this family maxim without so much as a glance at her nephew, as a cuirassier bestowed upon her a concupiscent leer, bringing a flush to her face. Auguste was perfectly mortified.

'Well then, I see ... I shall leave you to your bestial contemplation ... Good evening, Aunt.' And with that he set off for his headquarters, namely the Café Madrid on Boulevard Montmartre.

2

SO I STAY AT GRANNY SOIZE'S place when I reach the island and definitely not with my father.

Despite being his aunt, as the youngest child of a second marriage she is only eight years older than him. She never had any children of her own, but she had me.

To see her trotting about the village in her beige raincoat and little concrete-lacquered grey curls, you'd peg her as being between seventy-five and eighty-five years old. When this story started she was ninety-three. I'd just like to say that here on our island, where its residents enjoy both a healthy lifestyle and strong community ties – you eat what you grow in your own vegetable garden and everybody has their nose in their neighbour's business – there's a national record number of centenarians. With her ramrod posture, she dresses to the nines even just to go out for bread; her principal motto has always been maximum dignity at all times. You'll see her at 9.30 am at the bakery, 9.45 at the minimart, 9.50 at the newsagency to pick up her copy of the *Ouest-France* paper and at 10 o'clock at the cemetery to give her best to the family.

They say she had one great love, the sort of love that only comes along once in a lifetime, but that he went to sea and never returned.

The day has been long
Her eyes are weary
Of looking out to the ocean …

Well, that's what people say, or at least, it's what she always would have people believe, but I suspect her of sharing the local women's general opinion of the males of the species, a view both realistic and resigned: drones whose only purpose is that of making babies.

From the point of view of temperament, she's not one to be coy in her opinions to anybody who cares to listen, as she tends to think most people have tickets on themselves and completely lack modesty. With age and the mathematical absence of future which that implies, her lack of filter makes her borderline unmanageable.

They say that I take after her in this respect. No doubt that's the reason I have no boyfriend, not just the fact I'm a handicapped single parent. I'm not what you'd call a stunner, that much is true, but nor am I that ugly: I'm of average height and well-toned because of my crutches, I've got a good head of hair that I wear in a chignon, an open face and my mother's pretty blue eyes. And when I walk, a sailor once told me I reminded him of the lazy pitching and rolling of a yacht on a shimmering sunlit sea – which, you'd have to admit, is a pretty cool description.

Physically, it seems, I take after Rose, my real grandmother, Mamie Soize's half-sister and my father's mother, who died well before I was born.

In the '30s, on a day thick with a fog you could cut

with a knife, this woman distinguished herself with some extravagance by saving a score of sailors from a merchant vessel that had run aground. She leapt into the water fully clothed and, using the strength of her arms alone, dragged ashore what remained of an enormous lifeboat in which they had all sought refuge. Postcards from the time commemorating the event are available for sale at the newsagency. It shows Rose in her traditional Breton dress and bonnet, her chest bedecked with awards. When I was little, the adults in my life predicted I would look a lot like her, which I took as a compliment seeing as I thought she was really very pretty. Except that it wasn't my grandmother who featured in those photos. The photographer must have thought that a woman of character was incompatible with the graciousness befitting such an event, because he chose some inane beauty from the island to pose in her place, with her medals.

In fact, there remains only one photograph of that valiant Bretonne. It shows her standing next to her husband, beaming, because unlike me and Granny Soize, my grandmother Rose was madly and happily in love. It's true she had a slightly don't-mess-with-me air about her in the photo and there is a family resemblance, but it's my grandfather who really catches your eye: a scrap of a man like you see only in the colour plates of war-era medical books. An old cripple from the war of 1914–18, whom they'd set on a barrel because he was missing his legs, and part of his face too. Renan de Rigny: the perfect illustration of our island proverb concerning the scarcity of men: *If you find one, sink your hooks in, there won't be enough to go round!*

So, it is to this World War I veteran that we owe such a curious family name, whereas everybody else from these parts never ventures far when it comes time to marry, with almost all of them being called Cozan, Botquelen, Tual, Miniou, Malgorn or Jezequel. That should have told me something but there had never been any doubt cast as to our sense of belonging to the community: we always took our turn peeling vegetables at the village fêtes, went to all the funerals, and knew of every falling out that had ever taken place for the last thousand generations. This was where we came from, and that was all there was to it.

'So, how is that daughter of yours, Juliette?'

It's always the same conversational opener with Granny Soize when I arrive, even though she's unstoppable on WhatsApp and is always chatting to my daughter. I think it's because she only understands one in every five words of whatever it is you're saying to her over the phone, seeing as she's deaf as a post, but she's too vain to admit it.

'And you? How are you?'

'I'm very well. I've been put in charge of reprographics, but I think I've told you that plenty of times, haven't I?'

'Nothing ever changes with you, does it? But are you at least getting out and seeing some people?'

'If by *people* you mean *have I found a guy to look after Juliette?*, the answer is no. I don't need one. I've got quite enough people around with my friend Hildegarde and her family. And then there are my neighbours. The sixth floor of my building is the same as it is here; it's like a little village.'

Let's deal with my disabilities. After three super-painful operations at the ages of sixteen, eighteen and twenty-one and a series of metal plates later, I have a very damaged spinal cord. That's what makes walking so tiresome. It means I can only stand up with orthoses that attach to my legs and go all the way up my thighs, and I need two sticks to help me walk. I'm in constant pain, but because Granny Soize was a tough cookie and I used to get called a cry-baby, I learnt not to complain, to the point that now I don't even know if I feel any pain anymore.

Everything was fine provided I was doing rehab or I was back on the island, but when I had to confront real life on the mainland, the pile of adolescent bullshit married to the binary thought patterns of high school meant it was a whole different ballgame. No matter how hard I struggled to be a '1', with my crutches and legs in their braces, I was always a '0', a misshapen carrot always shoved aside because I didn't fall within the standard deviation. An ugly vegetable fit for the compost.

These days, nothing's really any different, even though I have a doctoral degree; adults are just more polite. People who don't know me just ignore me instinctively, as if I were incapable of giving anybody directions, of answering a question or having an opinion, just because I'm swaying on my crutches. It's as if I were some sort of retard, in fact. And if, by some miracle, they do talk to me, their eyes are fixed on some zone at chin level so as not to have to meet my gaze because they're afraid. Of what? Who'd know? I guess I might be contagious after all. Or bring them bad luck.

I won't dwell on my father's birthday dinner, which was held the evening I arrived and was of little interest in itself. What happened next, however, proved to be the starting point of this entire affair.

Dinner was rapidly polished off. Granny Soize had prepared some fried potatoes with mackerel in mustard and a simple Savoy teacake that my father had put away with not so much as a word of thanks to her or any attempt to get off his backside to lend her a hand, all the while boring us to tears with his conspiracy theories along the lines of: *we're being lied to – they're all rotten to the core – I know somebody who …* And I sat there nodding along with the customary tolerance of a woman who knows she's about to split, which I wasted no time in doing the minute the table had been cleared.

I headed out to see who was around.

Two sleeping sheep swayed backwards and forwards on their hooves in the darkness and a few cats on the hunt for scraps were making a bit of a commotion, but otherwise there was no sign of life in the village centre, apart from the Kastel, with its illuminated front window casting a rectangle of light onto the footpath. It has to be said: there's such a mournful atmosphere on the island in the off season that there'd really have to be a good reason not to flee back to the mainland. You might think that tourists would be discouraged by the feel of the place; on the contrary, it's what attracts them. In fact, it's the season of choice for those depressed souls who come looking for some authenticity, seeking to recharge their batteries by exposing themselves to the rocky outcrops, the wild seas and the endless rain.

The Kastel Bar is more than two hundred years old and people say the island's general state of contentment or unhappiness can be measured by the volume of alcohol consumed there. Regardless, it is definitely worth a visit, if only to admire its décor.

The owner – whom everybody knows by the classy moniker *the Boche's son*, after his father, *the Boche*, conceived under the Occupation – has covered his walls with hideous posters of the Breton version of the Paris-Roubaix road cycle race – the Tro-Bro-Léon – each featuring a muddy cyclist in different positions … with a pig. You'll also see lots of models of little pigs scattered about here and there, which must form part of some more extensive collection.

I greeted everybody there and plonked myself in a corner with a glass of cider as I interrogated *the Boche's grandson* – fifteen years old and already one elbow on the zinc bar – about the general state of despondency: the Stade Brestois football club had just suffered yet another humiliation.

As for the faces, they were always the same. There was Brieg, who fancied himself as a great skipper, with his traditional cotton tagelmust scarf wrapped around his neck. *They'll be coming to get him soon.* Who? To go where? Nobody's ever known! And Roger Orion, with a face the colour of raw steak, grumbling about … That particular night it was the fish-guzzling seals that he dreamt of picking off (and which he did, by the way, pick off) with his shotgun; bugger the marine park! And then there was Lebivic, the local reporter from the *Ouest-France*, whose most recent feat had been to print the list of losers as the winners of the local elections. And *the heron*, who used to be a DJ at the island's old nightclub, which closed in the '90s after repeated instances of people falling into alcohol-induced comas under their asbestos ceiling.

Obviously, the three Parisians had also made an appearance and were enjoying their big moment of fraternising with the natives – especially the depressed one with glasses, who was in full catharsis mode. Completely hammered, he was busy describing to a handful of louts in revolting, explicit detail how his girlfriend, Alice, had died when a stone stupa had collapsed on her.

Brieg, engaging in diversionary tactics, was insisting that when *they come to get him* he would be stopping over in Kathmandu – it was all planned – and he'd help those poor people dig a well. He'd already dug one in his garden, which meant he'd been able to water his potatoes the previous summer when the local council had implemented water restrictions. Roger Orion made the very pertinent observation that Kathmandu was 700 kilometres away from the sea and that furthermore it wasn't water they lacked, given they were at the foot of the Himalayas: 'The Nepalese couldn't give a shit about your well,' he'd added, unkindly.

The widower was explaining to them in a thick voice that his girlfriend had completely rejected all the fuckwits in her family – and they had returned the sentiment, calling her a leftie who didn't know how to maintain her social rank and who was letting the side down. *They're the reason she's dead*, he was wailing; because she'd had to flee to the other side of the world in order to escape them.

The drunks commiserated, nodding their heads in furious agreement, on this dire day – if ever there was one – when Brest still wasn't going to make the first division.

The tall, plain girl had added that Lili, their dead friend, a fabulous, sweet, intelligent, generous girl – can we just leave it at that, I said to myself – would have dearly wanted her ashes to be scattered into the sea from the island's cliffs. So, even if they didn't have any ash to scatter, seeing as she had been – and I quote – 'buried by force', they had come to throw her favourite stuffed toys into the water instead!

'With any luck a seal will choke to death on a teddy bear,' Roger Orion had felt obliged to conclude.

I decided I'd listened to enough crap for one evening, so I finished my glass and went home to bed. But sleep wouldn't come; it was as if there were something crawling through my mind, preventing me from relaxing. A feeling of *Unheimlichkeit*, something strangely troubling. And when I finally did manage to fall asleep, I was woken almost immediately by an appalling nightmare.

Feeling hyper-anxious, I fumbled around for my smartphone to see what time it was, and because I had nothing better to do since I couldn't get back to sleep, I typed the following words into Google: *earthquake Nepal death member of parliament* and brought up dozens of hits: Alice de Rigny, daughter of former MP and businessman Philippe de Rigny, had died 40 kilometres outside Kathmandu in horrific circumstances.

Alice de Rigny ... Philippe de Rigny ... Blanche de Rigny ... Suddenly I was wide awake.

I continued my search. Philippe de Rigny headed up oil trading company Oilofina. His son, Pierre-Alexandre, had just been arrested at Abidjan airport as he was about to board his private jet. He had been investigated for corruption in 2014 in relation to a matter involving the contamination of several city tips through the dumping of toxic waste. *Super Prick* was thus not a name that had been given to him lightly.

I got up and frantically started rummaging through Granny Soize's papers, hunting for any references to my family on my father's side. All I found was the photo of my grandmother and her sweet husband, which I knew about already, but this time I looked at it with fresh eyes. I had never appreciated, for example, how showy yet still somehow moving the image was: this tall, proud woman in her traditional dress alongside her old husband perched on his barrel, both of their chests festooned with medals, a pair of improbable butterflies pinned into their velvet case.

I was startled by Granny Soize.

'Do you get up this early in Paris too?'

'Tell me, did you know my grandfather?'

'What sort of a question is that to ask me at six in the morning? Yes, I knew him, but I was very young. When my sister used to come to the washhouse carrying him on her back, she would wedge him between two piles of linen so he wouldn't fall over. But because I was only knee high to a grasshopper and couldn't stop staring at the hole in his face, because his face was at exactly the same height as mine, they scolded me – and how that made him laugh … laugh and laugh … and believe me, that was terrifying!'

'You've already told me about that, but what I want to know is where he came from.'

'What do you mean *where he came from*? He came from here, of course!'

'Granny, *de Rigny* is not a name from around here!'

'Your grandfather was a bastard. The baby of a single mother, a Malgorn girl, which she had in Paris, where she'd gone to look for work. He was wounded in the battle of the Somme in 1916. His mother looked after him for years, but when it became too difficult she came back here to find him a wife who could take over the reins. He was already an old man and it was my sister he married. But she truly loved your grandfather Renan; apparently he was a very funny man.'

'I haven't ever seen Corentine's tomb. Will you show me?'

And after a visit to the bakery, the minimart and the newsagency, we found ourselves at the cemetery. The tomb, or rather the funerary chapel, of my great-grandmother, was right there at the entrance, a sort of small house to shelter her from the rain.

'Is that it?'

'Well, yes.'

'It's unbelievable!'

What I didn't add was that in that very mausoleum, away from prying looks, I had smoked my first fags and sniffed ether with my mates. Thank you, Corentine Malgorn, born 1850, for providing the youth of the day with shelter from the rain and refuge from their parents' gaze since 1924!

I ventured into the structure I knew so well.

Despite the fact that the memorial porcelain portrait had borne witness to all my youthful shenanigans, I'd never made the connection with anybody in my family. Corentine was not portrayed in the traditional white headdress and black outfit featured on all the other old gravestones, but instead was dressed as a chic, bourgeois woman.

'Looks like she clearly had means, then, if she could afford to have something like this built. But why did she have herself buried all alone and not with the other Malgorns in the cemetery?'

'Because they'd quarrelled, I think; ask your father, it's his grandmother, after all.'

I found him where I've always known he would be, next to his dinghy, quietly working away on his lobster pots. Though he's still a handsome man, with his bushy, satyr-like white eyebrows and leathery face, seeing him there I felt an immense wave of pity. He had fallen into a state of utter neglect, much like the fields on our island that have been overrun by brambles after feeding almost an entire community for centuries. His hands had grown clumsy, crippled by arthritis and nails that were too long, and his clothes were threadbare simply for want of any shop where he might buy anything new; of the internet, he knew nothing.

In a moment of weakness I wondered if it might perhaps be time to make our peace.

'What do you want for lunch, Dad?'

'Nothing. When are you leaving?'

'I'm taking the boat shortly.'

Silence.

Alright then.

I went on the attack.

'I wanted to ask you: why is your grandmother Corentine buried all on her own and not with the Malgorns?'

'Because she cursed them for a hundred years.'

'Why?'

'I have no idea, it's all water under the bridge now!'

'But why did she curse the Malgorns for a hundred years?'

'Since when are you interested?'

'Since today!'

'The Malgorns have always had tickets on themselves, that's probably why.'

'And what about your father? Why have you never spoken about him ...'

'He was an old cripple.'

'Yes, I know that, but where was he born?'

'In Paris.'

'That's what Granny Soize told me: that Corentine Malgorn had gone off to work in Paris, where she got herself pregnant to a de Rigny.'

He sniggered.

'She really gave those Malgorns something to talk about when she came back. Did you never wonder why we were the only ones with central heating?'

'No, because it never worked.'

'That Corentine, she brought a car across with her so she could drive her son around. A car ... In the '20s ... Can you believe it? There was only one road and she had a car! You can make her out in the background in Epstein's film *Finis Terrae*.'

'But who was he, this de Rigny?'

'What would I know ... The guy who knocked her up with a kid.'

'But did you never ask him?'

'Who?'

'Your father.'

'My father ... huh, and what mouth would he have answered with?'

'True!'

'Your problem is that you never stop to think before you speak! His birth certificate is at home in the drawer with the other important documents. Take it if you want to. Voilà ... voilà ...'

Voilà ... voilà ... He returned to fiddling quietly with his lobster pots, completely blocking me out, lost in contemplation of an oil slick on the sea. The rainbows forming on the water's surface must have reminded him of a similar slick somewhere off the coast of Valparaíso, Pointe-Noire or Pondicherry. I watched him in silence as he skittered mentally through the labyrinthine passageways of one of the ships on which he'd served, and then I headed back to his place … to our place … I don't really know what to call it: the place that has remained frozen in time since the day I left.

I ascertained from the muddled mess on his desk that he had not opened a single letter for a long time; bank statements, bills, letters from the mariners' pension fund and fishing-related advertising materials, all mixed together in great piles. Apart from that, there was nothing other than the detritus from an old sailor's life: photos of old crew members, postcards from distant ports, and business cards from bars and brothels at the ends of the earth.

He had once and for all renounced any participation in life's social structures – and I have to say, I envied him.

I had no difficulty laying my hands on the document in question, which was, paradoxically, tidied away in a drawer right next to both of our family record books. And then I got out of this place that had always freaked me the hell out.

I spent my remaining time with Granny Soize. We chatted a bit more about Corentine Malgorn. She didn't know much, except that she had opened a crêpe shop called The Greedy Seagull in Montparnasse in 1871, where Bretons would come to eat – refer to the postcard 'Little Brittany in the 19th Century', which is constantly reprinted: it shows my great-grandmother posing, young and proud, at the front of her establishment. When she returned to the island with the money she'd saved, she had built the most beautiful house in the village; the one in which I grew up and which my father was letting go to rack and ruin. My grandmother had changed the furniture in the '50s, a time when people swapped beautiful items for Formica, because it was magical the way it could be cleaned with the wipe of a sponge. Nothing remained of Corentine but a round porcelain portrait at the back of a lichen-covered mausoleum and an old clock covered in a bird-of-paradise design which had stopped working a long time ago.

Paris
12 June 1870

As well as taking courses at the Sorbonne, Auguste and his friends were busy reshaping the world in the fashionable cafés of the day. Much like their studies, this required serious expertise, the chief difficulty being knowing which café was in vogue at precisely the moment they planned to meet there. And one had to keep up, because a single man of letters or a sole politician could make or break the atmosphere of a place, dragging all his admirers along in his wake.

Currently, if one were a follower of Proudhon, Bakunin, Marx, Blanqui – or if one merely wished to bring down the Empire while discussing the suffering of the people – the Café de Madrid on Boulevard Montmartre was the place to be. One arrived after the casual passers-by had departed, never before 5 o'clock of an evening. One would hang one's hat on a peg and then order half a pint or an absinthe, scanning the crowd to make sure there wasn't an informer from the Department of General Security eavesdropping and trying to gather information. And then one would engage in conversation, refining one's arguments as one parried with others, and one's evening, indeed one's entire night, would be consumed by discussions. And one had to know how to use one's elbows, because generally speaking there were twice as many patrons crammed in as there were seats – and that's not counting the women, of course, who much like children, as everyone knows, only ever nibble on their food while perched on a man's lap.

That evening, there was a journalist – an old, thin, sorry-looking bearded socialist – who, from his seat at a table surrounded by young people was providing commentary on an opinion piece to appear the following day in *Le Réveil*, on the topic of Article 35 of the 1793 Constitution and the insurrectionary duty of the people.

'*When the Government violates the rights of the people, insurrection is their most sacred of rights and the most indispensable of duties* ... I set out in my article the mechanics of rebellion; it is triggered when the people's capacity for the intolerable reaches the point where rebellion is the only possible solution. And we are almost there! This is where we find ourselves!' gesticulated the old revolutionary from '48 by way of emphasis.

'When we've torched everything, we shall rebuild a society that is fair and egalitarian. We shall confiscate the means of production from the capitalists and return them to the people,' thundered Perrachon, a young law student and friend of Auguste. A chubby-faced fellow, renowned for causing disruption at the Sorbonne.

Auguste intervened.

'But once you have them, these workers' cooperatives, they'll have no choice but to compete with each other in order to amortise the cost of their new machinery and produce tonnes of commodities irrespective of people's actual needs, and they'll then have to beg the state to declare war so they can liquidate their surplus. And so it will go, over and over, until the world explodes.'

The old Forty-Eighter started to laugh heartily.

'That's youth speaking, there, courting disaster! I've

lived through three revolutions, but I still haven't witnessed the apocalypse.'

Auguste found all these debates at the Café Madrid intellectually stimulating, and a world apart from the opinions of his own family, whose construction interests had, for the time being, tanked. Which was to say that, the last he had heard, his brother Ferdinand was spending every Sunday afternoon in the salon of the Reinach family, close friends of Adolphe Thiers, doubtless seeking goodness knows what form of advantage, almost certainly involving the accumulation of more wealth. It would definitely not be a first, because it was Thiers himself, when he was Minister for Public Works, who had championed the planned railway between Paris and Saint-Germain, and who had awarded the contract for the construction of the stations to his grandfather, and then to his father.

When the journalist from *Le Réveil* decamped, Auguste pulled up a chair at a table with Perrachon and Trousselier, a tall, dark-haired medical student with an enormous nose hanging over his walrus-like moustache.

These two friends from the university were a couple of years older than Auguste and had come of age when the previous conscription laws had still been in force, narrowly managing to take advantage of the regime of exemption from military service in return for payment of a sum of money. Their parents had paid what they'd had to in order for their respective sons to be exempted from military service and that had been the end of the matter. They were his two closest friends; he felt he could trust them.

'Where did you pull that from, that business about the end of the world?' asked Perrachon.

'From one of our Philosophy profs, a man from Alsace who translated one of Marx's texts, *The Fetishism of Commodities*, for us. It's a terrifyingly prophetic text about the mechanisms of accumulation and concentration of wealth. And with my family busy trying to buy me a man, the supposed philosopher in me is currently spending quite some time reflecting on the issue of wealth,' said Auguste, ironically.

'They're reporting in *La Marseillaise* that Bismarck is plotting with Kaiser Wilhelm to install a Prussian cousin on the Spanish throne because he wants to prod the French into declaring war against him,' commented Perrachon.

'Don't I know it; I'm reading the papers twice a day and not sleeping a wink.'

Trousselier interrupted to reassure his friend.

'Well, your sacrifice won't make a jot of difference when it comes to this war, which is entirely the work of speculators on both sides.'

'As you might imagine, this war is the last thing I want, but should I refuse to go, I'll be executed.'

'Rest assured you're not the only one in your class to find yourself in a jam. On Saturday morning I was woken by the heart-wrenching cries of my neighbour across the landing, who was clinging to her son as the soldiers came to round him up. His father stood there on the doorstep, his arms dangling slack at his sides, crushed by guilt at not having found a solution. A few months earlier he had paid half the price, namely 5000 francs, to a dealer in human flesh for a substitute who was refused admission on the grounds of tuberculosis just as he was to enlist: the medical certificate had been faked!'

'The poor man! Does it have anything to do with that story of the army surgeon that all the papers are talking about?' asked Auguste.

'Certainly does! The fellow wrote bogus certificates for brokers certifying sixty substitutes who didn't qualify on medical grounds. They found 70,000 francs at his place! Fat lot of good that does for my neighbour, I hear you say; it was too late for him, he was given his marching orders on the spot.'

Perrachon hesitated for a moment, then proceeded with a conspiratorial air.

'Well, lads, I'm going to tell you a good one, but you're not to repeat it to anybody because it involves members of my family ... do you promise?'

'Promise,' muttered the other two.

Perrachon hauled himself upright on his chair, adopting the pose of somebody about to deliver some tasty revelations.

'Having hunted for months for somebody to replace my cousin Camille, whom of course you know, my Uncle Henry finally unearthed a man. Before submitting him to the recruitment board for admission, he had to notarise the sale. In the time it took him to hail a carriage to take him to the notary, the man was snatched from under his nose. By some kind of miracle, he located another a few days later; a superb recruit, five foot eleven inches, a magnificent cavalryman. The whole family came to admire him, he was that handsome! He signs him up and has the man stay at his place until it's recruitment time so as not to risk going through the same drama. This fellow lives it up for two months, wanders around my aunt's salon in his undergarments when she's holding her Friday afternoon tea parties, scorches the tapestry work on the chairs with his tobacco, refuses to dine with the servants, snaffles the tastiest morsels, belches and farts away at the dining table as he regales them with appalling stories in his gutter language... And...'

And here Perrachon paused for effect.

'... and makes my cousin pregnant.'

'Your cousin? Which cousin?' asked Trousselier, enthralled.

'My cousin Pauline.'

'No!'

'Yes, indeed! The sublime Pauline. The very one! And ... he gives her syphilis. Wait, that's not even the end of the story... it continues! After making life hellish for the whole family, our man – when he finds himself before the recruitment officer – nonchalantly pulls down his coat to show off his superb tattoo from Toulon prison. Then off he goes, hands in his pockets, happy with his first down payment, and his board and lodging, on the hunt for another family of dupes.'

'And?'

'Well, my cousin left yesterday!'

'But that's awful!' said Auguste, horrified, his effeminate hands pressed to his lips.

'Have you tried Rue Piat?' suggested Perrachon.

'What's on Rue Piat?'

'There are these mysterious advertisements. Take a look...'

And the young man pulled two newspapers from the pile of dailies lying around.

'Look, there, down the bottom, it's in there every day.'

'*Serviceman entitled to furlough is offering to replace young soldier currently enrolled as a student: present yourself at 12 Rue Piat.*'

'*Several young men wishing to enlist in the army as substitutes: present yourself at 12 Rue Piat.*'

'Where's Rue Piat?'

'At the top of Rue de Belleville, between the Buttes-Chaumont Park and the customs posts.'

Auguste consulted his watch.

'If I take a carriage now, I'll make it before nightfall.'

The young man left without further ado and hailed a fiacre to take him to the address indicated.

The cab headed down Boulevard Poissonnière, then turned at Rue du Faubourg du Temple to head up to Belleville, as Rue Piat lay well beyond the invisible border drawn by Boulevards Strasbourg, Sébastopol and Saint Michel, which divided Paris in two, the wealthy on one side, the poor on the other.

Although he had never ventured so deep into these neighbourhoods, he was aware what living conditions

there were like since Haussmann's opening up of the city
and the dizzying increase in rents. Thousands of people
were crammed into rickety, overpopulated buildings or
makeshift dwellings amounting to little more than a pile of
clapboards, and all this in deplorably unhygienic circumstances. He knew the labourers who went to work in the city
centre every morning came from these neighbourhoods.
That they were exploited, lucky to be paid even three francs
a day, and their wives half that, when in order to feed and
lodge a family, a minimum of four francs was required for
a room in a slumlord's lodgings, even in Belleville.

He would have to have been blind not to notice the
hordes of scruffy children left entirely to their own devices,
the young girls being prostituted, the single mothers who'd
been impregnated by their master then dismissed from
their position, their sickly offspring clinging to their skirts,
all of them doing their best to linger on the edge of that area
where they might rub up against the wealthy and make off
with a few coins.

He would have to have been a fool not to realise that
something in society was not functioning as it should.

To display sensitivity to the distress of the poor in the face
of one's own good fortune was a matter fraught with com-
plications, and one his own family was evidently incapable
of comprehending, but Auguste found himself seduced by
the challenge. He could not deny his own social status and
the gap that might exist between himself and the proletariat
whose cause he was espousing; nonetheless, he was keen to
find a way to at least bridge that gap, through some form of

exchange or contact, even if he were unable to fill it entirely.

He was convinced it required people such as himself to consider how the most deprived might access an education, and most importantly how to assist them in freeing themselves of the Church … convinced that to be a member of the affluent classes would prevent him neither from thinking nor theorising in the name of those who were in economically too fragile a state to rise up in revolt: Étienne de la Boétie, Thoreau, Marx, Engels … they were all sons of the bourgeoisie, and yet they expounded dazzling notions of brotherly solidarity.

To be able to philosophise at length about the destiny of mankind! All well and good, except that his conscription problem was casting a shadow over his entire future, and preventing him from making any sort of plans whatsoever. It was becoming an obsession. It had got to the point where he could no longer spend time with young people his age without wondering what arrangements *they* had made … however, short of having the audacity to ask them outright, the topic of purchasing a man, an insurmountable paradox for a socialist, proved an impossible one to broach. Whenever he saw his family – itself no sinecure – it was worse: every conversation around the dinner table seemed to lead in one direction only: conscription. They would bring up some person or other and thoughts would turn immediately to their son and thus to his departure or to his exemption. They would start talking about the year ahead and would have to contemplate Auguste's absence, or worse his death, and there would be sobbing.

It felt as if he were damned.

He pondered all this as he took in the squalid hovels, their façades blackened by soot, rags drying in the windows.

He was yanked from his thoughts when the coachman halted the carriage on Rue de Belleville, any further progress along the carriageway proving impracticable. Auguste was forced to walk the rest of the way, but barely had he taken a few steps before he found himself gagging on the abominable stench of excrement and rotting carrion, causing him to stumble.

The address he had matched a grubby eating house: a regular there was known by everybody in the neighbourhood of whom he asked directions to be trading men.

Mister Anquetin received him into a cubbyhole of a room, where he was having his supper.

Small and thickset, his face cleanshaven and leaning more to purple than red, the hustler was busy devouring an enormous sausage with evident appetite and delight. A candle was burning next to him with a generous flame, as if it were being fed not just by its wax, but by the foetid, stale stench that emanated from the man and filled the room.

As Auguste, feeling nauseous, in a tremulous voice and with faltering words, explained his circumstances, the dealer would from time to time fix his feverish interlocutor with an amused, sausage-laden look.

'For 15,000, I have a man, five foot eight inches, a fellow from Anjou. Magnificent, he is. Already served,' he finished up, his mouth spattered with fat. 'He suffered a wound to his leg which led to his discharge, but he's perfectly recovered now.'

'My brother-in-law, who's in the military, has warned me off such types. Often, after appearing before the recruitment board, they have themselves declared unfit for service, asserting that in truth while their injury may well have healed, the limb in question remains weak, meaning they are no longer able to serve. Which means my family would lose their down payment and I would be given my marching orders.'

'Well then ... for the much cheaper sum of 11,000, I have a smaller fellow: four foot eleven inches, but if you tease up his quiff, that would do the trick. He has good feet, no varicose veins. I'd take 30 per cent. I need 500 francs to kit him out and pay for his tobacco and wine. You bear the cost of having the contract notarised. A third on signing which I keep. A second third on the day the substitute is accepted by the recruitment board. The last third a year after conscription on certification from his corps' administrative officer confirming he's fit for his post.'

'11,000 for such a small man, but that's an enormous amount ...'

Anquetin lost his patience and raised his voice.

'We're well past the point when fancy fathers could keep us dangling before they settled the deal. We'll be at war in a few weeks and parents of dandies like you will be begging me to sell them my midgets. For double the price.'

'I'm told that in Paris, with all the factories closing, there isn't such a shortage of men. That a day labourer working for three francs would largely prefer to be a substitute ...'

'Oh, is that right? They told you that? Well then, if it's that easy, why don't you go find yourself a worker who feels like getting killed in your place?'

'My father will never pay that amount,' said Auguste, his face buried in his fine, girlish hands. 'He has made provision for 10,000 francs for an impeccable recruit,' he added in a whisper.

He turned on his best puppy-dog eyes – more mortally-wounded-deer – but though this worked so well on his mother it served only to make the horse trader laugh.

'Seems to me life in the barracks won't be such a walk in the park the way you're carrying on like a witless girl. But what doesn't kill you makes you stronger, so they say!'

After swallowing his last mouthful of sausage, Anquetin wiped his mouth with the back of his sleeve and tossed off some final advice to Auguste with a malicious smirk.

'Careful on your way home. They say the neighbour-hood isn't safe.'

3

THE FIRST DAY OF APRIL, eighteen hundred and seventy-one at half past four in the afternoon.

The birth of Renan Astyanax de Rigny, of male sex, at the domicile of Clothilde de Rigny, at 43 Rue du 4 September, to Auguste de Rigny, student, of Saint-Germain-en-Laye, aged twenty-one years, son of Casimir de Rigny, and to Corentine Malgorn, farmer, of Brest, aged twenty years, daughter of Yann Malgorn, is hereby formally declared and acknowledged. This declaration is read aloud by the child's father and mother before Aimé Perrachon, student, aged twenty-two years, residing at 10 Rue du Port Mahon, Paris, and Albert Trousselier, aged twenty-three years, residing at 8 Boulevard de la Madeleine, Paris, witnesses by their signature to the said declaration, and in the presence of myself, the undersigned Civil Registrar.

My forebears Renan, Corentine, Auguste and Casimir, Auguste's university friends Perrachon and Trousselier, Clothilde de Rigny, the aunt in Paris who had taken him in ... With its restrained vocabulary and basic syntax, there was no better stylistic form in the world for setting out the contents of this formal document written in pen and ink.

Let's pick up the thread again, paying close attention.

Like so many other penniless women from Brittany, my great-grandmother, Corentine, would have taken advantage of the railways opening up the region and headed to the capital to seek work as a maid. She would have been taken into service by a wealthy bourgeois family, where she would have been impregnated by one of the male line, most likely the boy closest in age, Auguste. He would have taken her to his single aunt so she could give birth in the coolest neighbourhood of Haussmann's Paris, the Grands Boulevards, or in other words to his aunt from the *beautiful* people set. He would have formally recognised the child with his uni mates as witnesses and would certainly have given him the Breton first name Renan, but also the revolutionary, impossible-to-pronounce name of Astyanax, meaning *protector of the city* in Ancient Greek. Having delivered her child into the world, she appears to have opened a restaurant that same year … And all this in the middle of the Prussian occupation and against the backdrop of the crushing of the Paris Commune.

That is what I took from that old birth certificate.

Let me rephrase it for you …

You'll admit, the story I'd been served up didn't hold water for a second. And no need for a doctor of letters to work that out; you just needed to have read Zola's *Pot-Bouille*:

> So, it wasn't enough never to be able to eat her fill, to be the filthy, clumsy slattern, the subject of constant abuse by the entire household: the masters of the house then had to go

and fix her up with a child! Ah! The bastards! Except that she could not have said whether it was the younger or the elder of them, because the old man had forced himself on her again the night of Shrove Tuesday. In any event, neither of them could have cared less, now they had taken their pleasure and she was left with the pain!

The author then recounts the young maid giving birth with the same clinical attention to detail he might have used to describe an animal dropping its offspring.

She gives birth in her room under the eaves, alone and silently, for fear of being turned out of the house, and abandons her infant on the ground in the covered arcade of the Passage Choiseul, pleased to have had some good fortune for once in that nobody saw her do it ... And there you have the condition of maidservants in the nineteenth century. But never, ever would you flout the law of reproduction within one's social class. And yet Auguste de Rigny had committed this ultimate transgression on 1 April 1871 by recognising my grandfather and, moreover, by choosing that first name – because I really can't see a girl from my island in Brittany calling her son Astyanax.

Why did he do it? Was he trying to make amends for something, to make good a debt? Was it a political gesture? Could it have been all of the above?

And that wasn't all. Here you have a Catholic girl from Brittany, and supposedly a poverty-stricken one at that, who travelled a great distance from home to earn a living, who opened up a restaurant by the name of The Greedy Seagull the same year as the birth of her bastard son ... What money would she have had to invest in such a business, which was, if one were to believe the postcard Granny Soize showed me, quite a decent size? And finally, why did she feature on my grandfather's birth certificate as a farmer and not as a maid?

In that photo, which was dated 1875, Corentine appeared dressed to the same high standards as she was fifty years later in the portrait adorning her family vault: that is, impeccably styled and cinched into her stays. Even at that young age, she had the air of a triumphant businesswoman. It was hard to imagine her ever being in somebody else's service.

The explanations provided to me by my family made the whole story seem like a jigsaw puzzle whose pieces had been jammed in with a hammer: it made no sense. My head, or rather, my imagination, craved more. I told myself it was far from a coincidence that those Parisians had come to drown their teddy bears on our island in memory of a de Rigny; it was like some sort of unacknowledged truth that had simply been biding its time before exploding...

In the train on the way home, thanks to the Mormon website familysearch.com, which has been relentlessly scanning parish registers from around the world since the 1960s in order to baptise the dead, I was able to reconstitute the de Rigny family tree in exchange for a few euros and a couple of clicks.

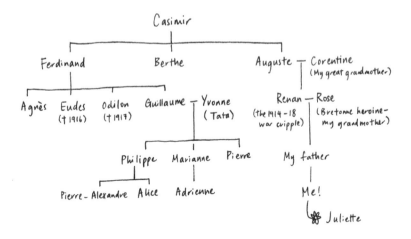

At its base, I put Casimir, the father of Auguste, who was the one who had acknowledged my grandfather, *the war cripple*. Casimir had produced three children, Berthe, Ferdinand – and the infamous Auguste. Berthe had not had any children, but Ferdinand had had four: one girl and three boys. It seems the women in the de Rigny family suffered genetic issues relating to childbirth, because Berthe was not the only one without any offspring; her niece Agnès, Ferdinand's daughter, had registered the stillbirths of five children in the parish of Saint-Germain-de-Paris. Of Ferdinand's three sons, two had died young during the Great War, one in 1916 and the other in 1917, without offspring. Only the last baby, Guillaume de Rigny, born in 1905, had survived. He had married a younger woman, Yvonne, who had given birth in about 1945 to our friend Philippe, otherwise known as *the Super Prick*, and then to twins Pierre and Marianne. Philippe had two children, Marianne one and

Pierre none. I didn't discover anything else regarding my putative great-grandfather Auguste. Nothing more about the son he had formally recognised on the official certificate I had in my possession, which seemed understandable given that the Communards had torched all the Parisian records of births, deaths and marriages that had been held at the Town Hall since the sixteenth century, as well as the duplicate records archived at Avenue Victoria; a political gesture intended to create a *tabula rasa* of bourgeois lines of descent and heredity. Nor was there any further mention of the date or place of his death which might have enlightened me as to his fate.

To Auguste's branch, then, I added the little limb which History had forgotten: us, the nobodies from Brittany, adding a pretty little flower at the end for my daughter, Juliette.

With the branch of Alice de Rigny – *the innocent tourist* – having been snapped off by the hand of nature's fury, I was struck by the scarcity of vegetation on that side. It consisted of only six people: Yvonne de Rigny *née* Guyot, born 1921, who, as you might say, had *one foot in the grave and the other slipping in*, her son Philippe and her daughter Marianne, both divorced, as well as their children, who were about my age, all born in the '80s. None of them had married nor had any children. Then there was Pierre, Marianne's twin, who also hadn't married or had any children.

It was the sort of tortured, sickly tree you find growing in barren soil.

In a few minutes I had identified almost all of them. There was the exquisitely wealthy centenarian maintaining her daughter Marianne and her granddaughter Adrienne, a jet-setting art photographer who, judging by her social media pages, appeared to be constantly coked up, wearing hyper-branded threads, and very, very stupid. In *the Super Prick*'s family, leaving aside the dead girlfriend, there was the father as well as the son, Pierre-Alexandre, both of them working for Oilofina and under investigation before the courts in the matter concerning the contamination of African waste sites, Pierre-Alexandre being recently resident in the Abidjan prison, Maca. Only Pierre eluded my investigative efforts, as I was unable to find the slightest trace of him on the internet.

The family owned numerous properties and a very luxurious 35-metre yacht, the *Sunday Morning*, whose every angle could be admired on photographer Adrienne's Instagram account, which featured some very fancy parties. When you scrolled through her photos, you could see the whole family took advantage of it, or had at some point, even the dead girlfriend ... And even the hipster dude with glasses whom I'd met, pissed, at the Kastel Bar – who, despite his left-leaning politics and his humanitarian aid work, nonetheless seemed right at home. Only Marianne, Adrienne's mother, caught in the background of those few shots, gazing into the distance through her squinting alcoholic's eyes, didn't really seem to be enjoying herself.

Paris
14 July 1870

For the second time that day Auguste had rushed to the newspaper stand at the end of his street, directly opposite the building site of the new Opera, in order to stay abreast of the latest developments in the saga of the Spanish throne and its corollary: war.

Forty-eight hours earlier, to appease France's fears of being encircled by Prussian monarchies, Kaiser Wilhelm I, who was taking the waters at Ems, had given his assurance in reply to the enquiry of the French Ambassador that his cousin, Prince Leopold of the House of Hohenzollern, would once and for all be withdrawing his claim to the throne.

Auguste had breathed again as he saw the spectre of conflict between France and Prussia dissipating.

But the nationalist press, with its bellicose pontificating, was pushing the Chamber to call for more: namely, that Wilhelm I go further and promise there would never be any other Prussian candidate. The Kaiser had replied that no further promises would be offered to anybody and that the matter of the Spanish throne was closed. However, the Ambassador had requested a new audience to seek such an undertaking. He had even gone so far as to pursue him on his morning promenade within the palace grounds. A magnificent caricature of this incident, portraying him abjectly tugging at the Kaiser's sleeve, appeared in the German press on the same afternoon of 13 July. The Ambassador had simultaneously sent a dispatch to Paris from the town of Ems in which he related this disagreeable affair. In it, he described how he, a close friend of Napoléon III, and France's representative, had been sent on his way like some nobody by a mere aide-de-camp, when he had simply come to put a perfectly legitimate request to the king of Prussia.

The previous evening, talk in the French newspapers had been of nothing but that dispatch, some declaring that war was the only solution to avenge the affront, others reporting that the worst had been averted, that all would be well and that the stock exchange had risen three points.

Leaning out of the window of his aunt's apartment, Auguste had seen his street invaded by hordes of students and workers yelling *Down with Prussia! To Berlin!* at the top of their lungs, and brandishing tricolour flags.

By nightfall, all Paris was out in the boulevards. Handkerchiefs were fluttering from windows and balconies everywhere, urging the demonstrators on. By morning, the streets had still not emptied and the country was unanimous in its desire to avenge the insult suffered by the French Ambassador.

By five o'clock that evening, the headlines of the dailies were of one voice when it came to the war – even *Le Figaro*, which described how the stock exchange had plunged since it opened ... And on top of all that, there had been no further news from his brother-in-law Jules since the latter had left for Brest to buy him a man. The recruitment board was meeting on the 18th; he had a mere four days left!

His friend Trousselier had managed to lay his hands on a booklet that was circulating illicitly at the faculty of medicine: *The Health Officers' Guide to Assessing Disabilities or Illnesses Rendering a Man Unfit for Military Service.*

'Take a look at it, maybe you'll find a way of getting yourself out of this mess,' he had said to him, offering him a little bit of hope.

Its introduction explained that *the army, as a result of the exhaustion, privations and dangers to which it would subject future soldiers, required a strong constitution, but also certain organic reserves from which to draw the necessary energy to battle poor weather, to endure deprivation and to brave obstacles and perils.*

'*Organic reserves*: what sort of a dreadful medical notion is that!' thought Auguste. Did the country not have any consideration for its sons, viewing them as nothing more than a store of organs to be endlessly drawn upon? And yet those young men whom he had seen marching in the streets could not wait to go to war against the Prussians. *To Berlin! To Berlin!* they were all shouting, those innocent, gullible young men; white-hot cannon fodder that would be hurled at the other side for the sole purpose of serving economic interests about which those poor fellows knew nothing. Generation after generation of families could be decimated in these slaughters, with mothers sometimes losing every one of their boys, and yet it seemed the whole world just put up with it – worse, brayed for it again and again – one historical cataclysm hard on the heels of another.

In addition to an impressive list of deformities that allowed conscripts to be exempted when called before the recruitment board – *goitre, tissue loss, chronic congestion, congenital idiocy, osteogenesis imperfecta, scrofula, rectal prolapse, supernumerary limbs* – there was also a long list of illnesses such as *syphilis, cancer, smallpox, tuberculosis* or *scurvy* which offered those afflicted young men the opportunity to die in their bed rather than on the battlefield.

Another passage read: *Abnormal ugliness resulting from defective anatomical composition which is likely to inspire repugnance and a degree of despair in the young soldier's fellow comrades shall be considered incompatible with military life where the majority of actions are shared endeavours...* No luck there, women found him very handsome, and, having acquired every possible malady as a child, he now enjoyed a cast-iron constitution!

So he would have to seek an escape route via the mental illnesses. The booklet distinguished madness which was visible to the naked eye: *torsion of limbs, loud delirium, erratic shouting, dribbling, incontinence* (in such circumstances there was no doubt as to illness), from invisible mental illness, which was very difficult to detect. Such cases required particular attention; behind such a madman one would often find concealed a fraud. Thus, it was appropriate to observe the subject when he considered himself alone, away from prying eyes. For this, it was necessary *to have him at one's disposal for some considerable time in order to make a definitive assessment, to provoke him into conversation, to probe him with varied lines of questioning, to ask him numerous and hurried questions pertaining to different subject matter so as not to allow him the opportunity to prepare his responses.* And if any uncertainty as to the diagnosis remained in the mind of the military doctor, this latter should not hesitate to employ *vigorous and painful means, provided however that such means not be excessively cruel.*

Auguste could not for a minute see himself launching into such theatrics, especially where it would involve his family, who would be summoned for interrogation as to his nervous crises. Just the thought of his brother Ferdinand in full flight before the recruitment board explaining what Ferdinand was already in the habit of calling his *leftist vegetarian deliriums* gave him chills down his spine.

That left homesickness. The booklet specified that this would only constitute grounds for discharge and not exemption, if, and only if, the soldier so desperately wished to return home that he was exhibiting *profound organic deterioration.* In other words, if there were nothing left in his poor organic reserves for the country to draw upon.

The regulation height of recruits had fallen fourteen centimetres since Louis XIV, owing to the numerous conflicts with England and Austria and especially those great consumers of young healthy males, the Napoleonic campaigns. Given the dearth of handsome, strapping lads, they'd become much less demanding: these days a young man had to measure five foot one inch, namely a minimum of one metre fifty-five centimetres, in order to be enlisted. Auguste stood at one metre seventy-seven. A magnificent dragoon.

One might wonder who, after this latest war, would be left in France to produce any babies with the women, apart from minuscule or mentally deranged men. And if these power-hungry butcheries were to carry on for some time yet, the much-vaunted beauty of *the French race*, of which national-ists of all persuasions were so proud, would be nothing but the stuff of dreams ... It was with these thoughts in mind that Auguste had closed the booklet, pondering the future of France.

4

HILDEGARDE.

My best friend. My soulmate, as fools like to say.

Whenever I go out with Hildegarde, we're taken for lesbians, doubtless because most people must think, as we're both abnormal – each in our different way – that if we're together, it could only be for mating purposes. Like animals.

Whenever I go out with Hildegarde, she's the one people notice, because she's got a pretty astonishing look with her very long hair, her magnificent Madonna-like face and her tracksuits, which she wears no matter the occasion, the only clothes capable of covering her overly tall body. Then people look at me, but their gaze doesn't linger because my crutches and legs with their orthoses make them feel vaguely sorry for me, and then they go back to her, telling themselves something's not quite right. And then they stare at her, trying to work out what it is; something to do with her size and her proportions ... and the little wheels start turning; the hard drive starts whirring: could I, couldn't I, am I disgusted, am I turned on? She couldn't give a shit, but the shamelessness of it all drives me crazy. In addition to her long limbs, Hildegarde has a neck like a giraffe and hands like spiders, plus all the things that don't work on the inside, but you can't see those.

I met her at the functional rehabilitation centre in Lorient where they sent me to learn how to walk again. We were sixteen years old and we'd both just been discharged from hospital, me after my accident and her following the umpteenth operation to straighten her spinal column.

The day I arrived, when they pushed me into the dining hall for the first time and into the free spot between two patients suffering from Duchenne muscular dystrophy, two young people, crucified in their wheelchairs and at the end of their life expectancy, I started crying so hard that one of the carers came to take me back to my room, where I curled up on my bed, my face turned towards the wall. Same thing the next day. And the day after that. After three days, an improbable creature stopped by, her head encased in a metal halo held in place by pins driven into her skull and to which were attached traction splints fixed into a plaster corset: a scene of pure medieval horror.

What's more, she was smiling, the idiot.

That's Hildegarde!

'Why are you crying?' she asked me with a hint of annoyance in her voice.

What was I meant to say to that? That my tears were a cocktail of shame and disgust at the sight of the disabled people around me. Of fear at being stuck in a wheelchair forever. Of anger at being lumped in with this freakshow. Of incomprehension at seeing them not in the least bit affected by their misfortune and here I was, bawling at the injustice … In short, it wasn't very pretty, as only real human emotions can be sometimes. Picture yourself suddenly disabled, especially at sixteen. I can guarantee your spirit would falter. It's not like playing at being armless, with one limb strapped behind your back, or being blind with a blindfold over your eyes; it has to do with feelings of impotence, being a tortoise on its back ... Banishment.

I looked at her, wide-eyed. When you find yourself in this sort of situation, a few centimetres away from a person with Marfan syndrome with nails fixed into their head, who is asking you in all seriousness *but why are you crying?* – you've got no reference point, because situations like that never happen in real life.

She called the nurse to have me put back in the wheelchair and she pushed me to the dining hall. It was fish that day, a Friday. Once again she put me between two people suffering from myopathy, saying to one of them, 'Come on, move your wheelchair,' with the same brutality that your regular teen would use to another. Then she sat down next to me. They served us prawns as a starter and everybody started laughing when the plates arrived at the table. At first I didn't understand why; then I realised that the quadriplegics, myopathy patients and amputees sitting around us couldn't peel them because their hands were too awkward, or useless, or non-existent. 'Make yourself useful!' Hildegarde said to me, and I started shelling the prawns in silence, my nose buried in my fingers.

With her perpetual cheerfulness, her simple good humour and her constant wish to make people happy, she served as my guide in my new world and after a fortnight

I was mucking about with the Duchenne patients just as I used to with the kids back home on the island. She helped me tame my new body. More precisely, she taught me how to sweet-talk into action that old wreck of a jalopy which, from this point forward, I'd be using for my onward journey. And none other. Never any other.

In short, when I felt ready to take all of that on, I left for boarding school and Hildegarde went home. We spoke often on the phone, and when I received my study allowance and my room at the university residence I left my island, because if I hadn't, who knows what else would have happened to me. And so I went to live in Paris, where she was living, and ever since we've seen each other almost every day.

Juliette.

My daughter with the big, bright, serious eyes.

One night when some old mates from uni were having a party in their apartment to celebrate several birthdays at once, I got so wasted I would have – and I use the conditional quite deliberately seeing as it's a hypothetical situation we're talking about – I would have completely blanked the fact I banged a guy standing up against the bathroom cabinet. In those days, I was scared of finding myself all alone in my little maid's quarters room, so I often went out and left parties much the worse for wear; I was almost always the last to leave, when there really was no more hope of anything happening. A month and a half later, I felt so ill I went to see a doctor, who told me just by looking at me: 'Come now, young lady, you're pregnant!' He sent me off for blood tests and when the lab technician told me he was right, I was stunned. That's when I did some cross-referencing and ended up with the day of that joint birthday party.

Somebody thinks they saw me disappearing into said bathroom, hence my inferred memory, but nothing could be less certain. It must be said that I'd had several other partners in the meantime; scars on my back, orthoses, ankle boots, mini-skirt, who knows why men have always found me sexy with my legs and their apparatus.

I sat down in the nearest café to the pathologist's rooms and called Hildegarde to tell her to come and meet me.

That's when, as I was waiting for her, some guy who must've been fifty to fifty-five years old, poorly shaven, wearing crotch-hugging jeans that showed off his bulging bits, a bomber jacket and red Converse sneakers came into the bar with his whingeing kid stuffed into some sort of hiking backpack and sat down at the counter. The child was wearing a mini puffer jacket and an enormous beanie that was falling down over her eyes and she was whining because she was too hot. Her father was trying unsuccessfully to bring his cup to his lips as the kid wriggled around on his back, her face flushed … waaaaa … waaaaa … It was unbearable! He knew perfectly well, the idiot, that he was irritating us with his kid … waaaaa … waaaaa … He was even more aware of the fact that before her birth he wouldn't have tolerated the situation for a second either.

With that kid carrying on just a few metres from my ears, I thought of my fatherless pregnancy and the fact

I would be facing the ordeal entirely on my own. I knew nothing about children. I was an only child, raised by an abrasive and impatient old aunt. I didn't know where I'd find the resources to give a child the attention and love it deserved.

'Is that going to go on for much longer?' his neighbour at the bar asked.

'She wants to get down —'

'Well, get her down!'

The guy undid his back contraption and put it on the floor with the kid still in it, squeezing her between his legs and the counter, amid all the sugar packets, the old metro tickets and the losing scratchies.

Waaaa … waaaa … And she was off again, even louder now.

I stared at the little girl, who was busy pleading for her father's attention. She was tugging on his jeans, and without even lowering his eyes he responded with little patting gestures like those you'd give your pooch. At one point he even picked up a copy of *Parisien* and started to read an article as he reached down with a piece of croissant, feeling around, trying to stuff it into her ear, thinking it was her mouth.

And suddenly I had a vision of my father and a sort of bitter bile rose up within, filling my mouth.

'You can do whatever you want to get his attention. He'll never look at you. All he wanted was to screw your mother, some pretty little piece of ass, no more than twenty-five years old, just so he could forget for a moment that he was mortal. You gotta understand, some young ass, it's good, it's sweet ... But now here you are and you're giving him the shits! It was still vaguely pleasant when you were a baby, it was cute, all that flim flam around your vintage cradle, but the fact you're growing up makes him even more aware of his own decrepitude and that's not so much fun anymore for the old man! The point is, you ruined everything, you're a burden! A weight he has put down on the ground in an attempt to try to remember what life used to be like without you for as long as it takes to drink a coffee. Life without a kid. And you put up with it without doing a thing. Do something, goddamn it; anything. Come on, you fill me with contempt. You're just a loser. But look at him, now he's actually having a laugh with the manager while you're there, your snout glued to his shins ... Waaaa ... Waaaa ... Down there in the dust.'

I know she read all of that in my look because she made a move. Finding an unexpected handhold at the bottom of the counter, she suddenly toppled over, doing a face-plant onto the floor. There was a harrowing scream, a bloodied nose – the works! She had managed to spoil her father's coffee and with a bit of luck his entire day once he brought her back home with a swollen face to be called *an irresponsible bloody idiot* by his younger other half.

'Congratulations, that's my girl! Just keep on irritating the hell out of him. Anything other than fucking up your own life by falling off a cliff!'

A daddy, a mummy, what the hell did I need with all that bullshit; what I needed was a loving, watchful helper. So, when Hildegarde finally arrived and found me limp and listless, I simply asked if she was ready to help me. She promised me that she, and especially her parents, who had already lost two children to Marfan syndrome, would always be there for us – and they always have been. What's more, they knew what to do.

Aunt Hildi will never be able to have a child, but she has Juliette.

It was Hildegarde who got me into legal reprographics, ten years ago now. Ten, that's how old my daughter is too, and it was precisely then that I drew a veil over my Icarian ambitions and the precariousness that went with them. In other words, when Juliette was born I stopped living any old how and got a real job. For her part, Hildegarde had been in reprographics forever and a day. Unlike me, she hadn't completed any studies and thought repro would be the ideal day job because the only thing in life that had ever interested her was her battle against animal cruelty and her dedication to the animal rights organisation L214. To hell with everything else. You could say she's built of unusually stern stuff to be able to cope with the unbearable cruelty of abattoirs and intensive farming, but when you know her well you're just struck by the extreme consistency of her temperament with her choices.

The work was on the list of so-called *reserved* jobs – that is, jobs reserved for the disabled, so donkey work – but it still needed to be performed with a high degree of conscientiousness given what was involved. Practically speaking, it consisted of scanning all documentation, page by page, relating to every major and minor indictable offence committed in the capital, apart from political or military crimes. I loved the work. I had the protected status of a civil servant, the salary wasn't terrible, and you could work at your own pace. And there was such a jolly atmosphere of *freaks* with a great sense of community, along the lines of *Appoint some disabled people, it's such a laugh seeing them work!*

The bulk of the work would arrive straight from police stations and the rest of it from the chambers of examining magistrates. All the questioning, the records of police searches and seizures, transcripts of phone intercepts, pinging and triangulation, DNA expert reports, autopsies, Facebook page captures, records from listening devices in cars, letters rogatory of every kind: these piles of police paperwork appeared in our office to be digitised and stored on CD-ROM for the lawyers so they could prepare their clients' defence.

A few months before the start of this saga, I was promoted to team manager and I only had to manage the data and dispatch the work. I was based on the Île de la Cité, where they handled indictable offences, and every now and then I would drop in to Boulevard des Italiens to visit my friend Hildegarde, who was assigned to white-collar offences.

Once the file digitisation was completed for the week, we might duplicate a few CD-ROMs to read at home on the weekend, like you would a novel. Hildegarde found it more entertaining than television shows like *Faites entrer l'accusé* or *Complément d'enquête*. For my part – if the cops transcribing the statements had any sort of artistic sensibility – it would remind me of those nineteenth-century novels I was so fond of and which I'd studied in such detail for my thesis, *Social Rancour and the Proletariat of the Quill in the Nineteenth Century*. Much like them, they would recount the unremitting effects of greed on the fate of their characters: bankruptcy, jealousy, fraud, unexplained wealth, unlawful acquisition of an interest, misappropriation of public funds, despoliation, tax evasion – all they ever talked about was money.

The author Octave Mirbeau, who at some point in his life had a job similar to mine, had one of his characters say:

> I would copy out the registers at the notary's office and be intrigued by the endless procession of acts of passion, crimes and murders inspired by man's desire to own a field.

Well, I got the same feeling from reading those scanned proceedings. Dealers would beat each other up over a swiped bar of hash or a territorial dispute; somebody would torture for a credit card PIN or kill for a handbag ... And the happiness you thought was warranted by the superiority of your spirit was to one day own a Porsche Panamera with all the bells and whistles so you had bragging rights outside your housing block. In the supposedly astute criminality on display at Hildegarde's office, the violence was perhaps not quite as obvious, but its consequences could prove considerably more devastating, with the shutting down of companies, staff hung out to dry, or millions in VAT fraud. The objectives were still more or less the same: parade around in a Porsche at Gstaad or in the streets of Blanc-Mesnil. I couldn't tell you which was more vulgar.

Those hungry for sensationalism would immediately conclude that the two of us were making money from the files we got hold of which were making a splash in the media:

> Where could the leak have come from? How did journalists get their hands on documents from an investigation that were subject to confidentiality, despite nobody else having had access to it? An enquiry has just been launched by the public prosecutor.

Everybody was open to suspicion – judges, cops, lawyers – but who for a second would have suspected the two halfwits from reprographics? Definitely not the inbred judge with the narrow shoulders covered in dandruff who supervised our department and whom you'd see once a quarter at most. In the unlikely event we were suspected, there would have been nobody better placed than the two of us playing the mentally deficient. It was so unoriginal.

As for the interview records of those people paid thirty times the minimum wage who didn't even know the address of their place of work or of those comfortably housed in company apartments with parquetry floors and moulded ceilings for the rent of a place in a suburban housing estate – fans of the *droit du seigneur* or merely those who used their position to subsidise their restaurant meals, their taxis, their renovations or their electoral campaigns – we never took advantage of any of those sickening transcripts. Firstly, because with our overly recognisable physiques we would have been busted in no time when we showed our faces to carry out the transaction. And secondly, because the press didn't even have the means to pay its journalists appropriately, so you can imagine what they'd pay their sources …

So, Hildegarde and I didn't sell them, but from time to time we might have slipped them into an envelope addressed, for example, to *Le Canard*, or to *Libération*, *Mediapart* or to *Le Figaro*, depending on the political stripes of the subject of our opprobrium. We would do it just out of malicious delight, to see how it sowed the seeds of panic in people busy running around a stack of dominoes they had spent months building and which was in the process of collapsing before their very eyes. To watch the little black rectangles fall with no more effort required than that first flick, each domino bringing with it another one twice the size as it all came tumbling down. We had a blast watching these chain reactions of disgrace and the heads that went rolling into the sawdust. Enthralling soap operas that kept us on the edge of our seats for weeks. Better than a Netflix series. We had ourselves some pretty sweet TV dinners there on my girlfriend's sofa, watching the news on loop.

Brest
14 July 1870

If there had not been any sign of life from Jules for the preceding three weeks, it was because he was having a fine time entertaining himself.

Ah, Brest!

Brest and her twenty-five thousand soldiers. Brest and her one thousand prostitutes. He was convinced that even the sea breeze in Brest had something of a whiff of vulva.

When there had been discussion of someone being sent off to find a man to buy for his numbskull of a brother-in-law, he had immediately volunteered, spying an opportunity to get away from the de Rigny family. He had suggested Toulon, but his wife, Berthe, had vetoed that idea, saying the place was too dangerous. So, on the pretext of having friends there, he had proposed Brest, which was quite some distance from Paris yet had a direct train connection.

Jules had always frequented whorehouses and he had to admit it had not been the same for a number of years now. The notion of a seminal drain where one would go to satisfy one's physiological needs was no longer alluring. The modern man was looking for *new offerings*; he wanted *to be listened to*, he was looking for *Love*. Everyone wanted their working-class girl, their own little *grisette*, fourteen to nineteen years old, in her cheap furnished apartment, and preferably with her mother around to keep her clean.

As for the brothels, with their trinkets and *chinoiseries*, their wall hangings and their scrubbed girls, they had become so desperately petty bourgeois. Jules found it all profoundly unappealing, rugged man that he was, used to the virile atmosphere of the garrison.

His thing was the streetwalkers: those grubby girls who would stand next to building sites and vacant lots and lift their petticoats in the shadow of the walls of Paris. Their animal odour, their slovenliness, reminded him of his own primitive self, his lost barbarism. Girls like that were to be found everywhere in Brest, by the hundreds even, in the Seven-Saints quarter or perched on the ramparts. They were even in the fields, where they set up signs with their name. He was especially fond of the girls from Léon. Their earthiness, their simple nature so characteristic of Bretonne peasant girls and accentuated by the fact they understood barely three words of French; all of it he found enormously exciting. He also found them more spontaneous, less mechanical than the Parisian girls, who made it a point of honour to let you know how bored they were while you were screwing them. A Léon girl, for her part, displayed an apparently sincere erotic delight. And all that quite cheaply. No, truly, Jules was keeping himself most entertained.

At the end of his three weeks of debauchery, a letter that had been left for him at the hotel's reception called Jules to task: *What progress has there been in the purchase of Auguste's replacement?* he was being asked by his father-in-law.

It wasn't like him, but it was true that in this affair he was dragging his feet.

Jules was the sort of man who considered war to be the most handsome manifestation of human intelligence. War and the army. They were the only two things that managed to corral and guide men, to provide them with action, rules, a purpose. Consequently, he found the notion of seeking a substitute for Auguste a detestable one, when military service would do him the world of good. He said he loved the people, did he? Well then, let him have to put up with them for nine years in the army and let's see how much he loved them then! But he was nonetheless prompted to make an effort because of his dear, sweet, poor Berthe. Were she to lose her brother in the war, she would equally lose her mind, given her already somewhat weakened state after her third miscarriage. What's more, his father-in-law had given him 11,000 francs; having already spent 1000 on various orgies, were he by some miracle able to find a man, he would offer him 8000 and could then pocket the difference himself. All he had to do was bring the substitute straight to the recruitment board so he could be approved and nobody would think of asking him for a record of account. And as for payment of the balance in respect of said replacement, well, let's see in a year from now; in war, anything could happen.

So he set his convictions to one side and made for the doorman of his hotel, a fellow with a mind like an archive of crime who had proved himself more than helpful in the matter of prostitutes. He would surely have some advice for him on the subject of the sale of men, being a somewhat similar matter.

'I need a handsome type by the 16th, somebody with good teeth and of irreproachable moral fibre. I'm aware there's not much time, but my young brother-in-law's recruitment board meets shortly and there must be no risk of his being turned down. There'll be no further options at that point except to find a man of his height in the week following his enlistment. He's 1 metre 77 centimetres tall, you can imagine the problem...'

'But, Monsieur, the war is almost upon us, they're talking of calling up the reserves.'

'Yes, and? This blasted war, it's just a formality! Did you read what Leboeuf has been trumpeting: we're more than ready, our army is prepared down to the last pair of boots and britches. And the chassepot rifle – I've tried it myself: an extraordinary breech-loading weapon – and what a range! 1700 metres! A marvel. Those Prussians will be shot down like guinea fowl! Find me a man and I shall pay well.'

'You won't find anybody. The touts from the replacement agencies have emptied out the whole Finistère region.'

'Any other ideas, then...'

'The islands.'

'What do you mean, the islands?'

'Nobody ever goes looking for men on the islands because it costs too much.'

'But is there anybody there?'

'Three thousand souls. You have to make the journey by sailing boat, and it's dangerous.'

'Well, find me a boat.'

5

ONE DAY, WHILE I WAS dealing with the file of a lawyer who had been worked over by his clients, I came up with the idea for my little business.

I had never come across a case like that before, and as I know quite a few people, at least by name, I was curious to know who had been beaten up. I was on my break, so I took the chance to flick through the file as I sat there on my stool.

The victim had told the cops how the dealers had come to his office to extract one of their mates' files from him. He had of course refused, concerned about possible reprisals on snitches, whose details generally appear at the top of statements: *your name is such-and-such, you live at* ... So, the dudes beat him up and turned his entire office upside down trying to find the CD-ROM in question. Since that sort of digitised document is incomprehensible if you're not familiar with legal jargon, once they found it they asked the lawyer to print them out the pages with the lists of users that the police had pulled from the guy's mobile. The truth was they hadn't come to avenge their mate but simply to pick up his deals where the latter had left off after his arrest.

Working in reprographics, I used to photocopy dozens of lists every week in the drug squad files, but I had never put a commercial value on them. Suddenly it seemed so blindingly obvious that I wondered why nobody had ever thought to make money from this manna from heaven.

So it was following this discovery, when I was back in my little room under the eaves after putting Juliette to bed, that I started systematically sifting through all that sludge in order to extract my first batch of material.

I charged 1000 euros for a list of 100 contacts, which was really very cheap. Let's imagine that just half the numbers from an address book are active and the owner of one of the numbers buys on average 40 euros of cocaine or hash per week; one number would have paid for itself in a week, and a dealer could keep a customer for two years who might bring in others. Sometimes I had huge numbers and I made over 3000 euros in one hit, but generally speaking the phone seized from a dealer wouldn't have more than fifty or so names. We're talking here about an ultra-perishable commodity, because drug users constitute a very volatile clientele. Driven by an MO of urge/frustration, they'll change dealers at the drop of a hat if they don't immediately obtain the product they're craving, and their number won't be worth a thing anymore. So you had to be super-quick ... And following my promotion, because I was the one responsible for dispatching the paper files, it was even faster: as soon as a file from the drug squad passed through my hands, I had it scanned as a priority. Then in the evening, because it was also my job to close up at work, I would duplicate the CD-ROMs I was interested in and take them home.

In four years, I had drawn up an Excel spreadsheet with about fifteen thousand mobile phone numbers, organised according to different criteria: details of the drugs used, the suppliers, the quantities consumed and, most importantly, when the purchasers were brought into the station to snitch on their dealer I would make a note of their real name (and not just *Fred 32*, *the blonde chick* or *the black guy*, as they appeared in the list of contacts). There was no doubling up and I had quite a few addresses of well-known figures who were systematically brought in; the cops love nothing more than to feast their eyes on the celebrity set pissing their pants. It was all saved to the cloud. Now, with a bit of hindsight, I'm wondering why I wasted so much time drawing that thing up. I think you'd probably have to ask those weirdos in the United Sates who stockpile firearms. (I'm very hard on myself.) Whenever they're asked what they're going to use the arsenal for, they always give the same answer: they want to be ready. For what? Not even they know. If you want my opinion, it allows them to tell themselves that if they wanted to they could show people what's what, with their gun-racks filled to the brim. A sort of narcissistic reassurance in a world where they feel disempowered about the fact they've got no control over anything. Similarly, this cloud of mass destruction was there to reassure this tortoise on her back, so she could tell herself that she could create one hell of a shitshow if she ever felt the need.

Shady activities require the services of loyal men and women, united by similar backgrounds, so we kept the work in-house, as it were.

My business partners, Ahmed and Mohamed, came from across the landing. The two of them, Dupont and Dupond as I affectionately called them, were the sort of Arabs you invite to improve diversity at parties in Paris because they're gay, elegant and cool. When I put my cunning idea to them, they looked at me in genuine wonder. One of them said to me: 'Too good!' The other: 'Too cool!' They knew a lot of people and so didn't have any problem flogging my lists to dealers with a margin which I suspected was totally over-the-top, but I didn't give a damn because what mattered to me was being able to work with people I trusted who were in it for the long haul, which has always been the case. I also knew they would do everything to ensure nothing could ever be traced back to them; as for tracing it back to me, that was unthinkable.

In order to launder my money, I first started doing business with Dioulou, the Malian father of a family on my floor (second door to the left of the toilets), whom I paid cash.

If immigrants are only perceived by their capacity to harm it's because they are seen first and foremost as a burden on the receiving populace. Dioulou and I, however, had developed a system of perfect osmosis, of brotherhood, which really ought to serve as a model, because it allows everyone to help themselves while being mutually beneficial.

Have you never noticed the black guys dressed in parkas three times too big for them, wearing worn-out sneakers with no socks, zigzagging on their bikes through Paris with a freezer bag on their back? They're illegals and that phone attached to their handlebars doesn't belong to them.

Somebody ordering a hamburger and fries pays for delivery via their mobile through the platform and then the platform credits my account as the official owner of the courier business. Then I reimburse Dioulou in cash for what I legally make every week, worked out to the last cent. He's delighted, because he has a job and a salary without necessarily having to have the residence permit that goes with that, and it allows me to launder my money. After Dioulou with UberEats, there were his cousins, Dembelé and Diara on Deliveroo, because I'm hyper-legit and don't make any margin on them using my account. And then, when they started carrying out inspections, they all switched over to Stuart. When Dioulou got his papers, he became an Uber driver and I bought him a car that he rented back from me. I was what is known as a 'micro-entrepreneur', a disabled sole-trader with quite a lot of work. Who had three internet bank accounts, two bikes and a crappy car driven around by Malians 24/7.

I've never felt guilty about bringing in some extra dough like this. Firstly, because with the 1,320.92 euros net per month that I got from the Ministry and the 900 euros of rent I had to pay for my 12 square metres, I couldn't get by, mainly because of the taxis I had to take to get around this bitch of a town, which is not at all disabled-friendly, and because of the private school my daughter attended so she wouldn't drag a string of losers around behind her. And also because after an exhausting day, when Juliette is asleep and it's nice outside, I like sitting on our little balcony with a joint so I can forget the pain in my back for a bit without anybody coming and giving me grief.

To those right-wing critics who would accuse me of not playing by the economic rules or who'd try to prevent me living the way I live, to the good people of the left who, for my own good, would be tempted to preach to me or bombard me with idiotic health warnings, I would reply that when an offence has no victim – if nobody's body, property or rights are threatened – well then, it's the Regime you're trying to protect and I've had the shits with the Regime for a very long time now … And to the best of my knowledge, I'm not the one who enacted those rubbish micro-entrepreneur regulations … And for god's sake don't anybody come talking to me about drugs or public health, given what we eat and have to breathe every single day.

Like everybody else, I had my dreams: a pretty apartment for the two of us with a balcony and most importantly a lift, because hauling yourself up six flights when you're disabled is seriously like the Stations of the Cross. I could have lived on the ground floor, you'll say to me – I did that when Juliette was born, I swapped my maid's quarters for the dismal concierge's rooms, but when she was old enough to climb the stairs, we went back to living up there.

As a child growing up, America was the only thing on the horizon when I looked out from my house, so I find it impossible not to have some sort of view, to have a window looking straight onto another building. From my miniscule apartment, when we stood on that tiny balcony and craned our neck a little, we could see the Seine. And since the skies of the capital are filled with seagulls from who knows where because the fish have dried up, it just about does the trick.

And there was no question of living in a less expensive arrondissement – quite simply because everything is concentrated in the centre and spread out in the suburbs. We had everything conveniently below us which is essential when you can't get around.

I had another one, another dream. The particularly light and chic Japanese titanium exoskeleton which I use these days and which I'd spotted back then on Instagram. It cost me a bomb and there was lots of to-ing and fro-ing to adjust it and learn how to coordinate my movements. Fortunately I had a little helping hand on the financial front, thanks to looking after Tata Yvonne, because otherwise I would have had to sell quite a few of them – my lists that is – to be able to afford such a thing. Thanks to that device, I can finally get around after Juliette instead of always feeling rooted to the spot, clinging to my crutches as I watch her get further and further away, letting her think it doesn't bother me.

That business is the only secret I've ever kept from Hildegarde. Well, she's far from stupid, she got a good view of the CD-ROMs spread out all over the place when she used to just turn up unannounced or when she brought Juliette home. She always sensed there was something not quite right. Once she even picked one up from the floor and grilled me to test my lies, but the restraint she showed in her interrogations always had me believe that she was never doing it to throw me, but just to satisfy herself that my little fictions would hold water, just in case.

It wasn't that I was scared she would judge me; far from it. If I never said anything to her about the drugs at the time, it was just because I was worried she would hassle me to donate to her animal welfare association all the money I was barely managing to put aside, cent by cent. The fact is there has never been any room in her life for anything except her commitment to that cause, and because of her condition, because her time is limited, she's not about to waste it prevaricating. In other words, when Hildegarde wants something, she knows how to be very, very annoying.

But then something suddenly happened that threatened ... I don't know how best to say it ... that basically screwed up my daily routine and in the process ruined my plans. The official opening of the new Palais de Justice court building, which nobody ever thought would get off the ground, had just taken place after all, and what they were calling the historic move to Batignolles from the Île de la Cité site as well as from six other locations, with its one thousand three hundred trucks and one hundred thousand boxes had started. They had planned an initial slowing down of activity covered by the jurisdiction in the former Palais de Justice where I used to work. Then there would be a second phase, in which business was supposed to pick up progressively over a fortnight up to 30 per cent at Batignolles, before the third phase where business would be back to 100 per cent, concluding once and for all the separation between the two sites: the Tribunal de Grande Instance, that is, the court of first instance, out in the sticks at the Porte de Clichy, with the Court of Appeal in the centre of Paris.

It was said that bringing together in one place military hearings, cybercrime and anti-terrorism matters on the one hand and organised crime and financial crimes on the other would, for prosecutors, completely transform both national security and the fight against money laundering. The île de la Cité reprographics department would thus merge with the financial crowd from Boulevard des Italiens, and Hildegarde and I would finally be working together. It all promised to be magnificent, efficient and so on and so forth, except that access to this Babylonian structure only remained possible via the miserable Line 13 of the metro, where orange-vested 'pushers' already had to cram passengers in and the courts weren't even open yet.

With an additional fifteen thousand people every morning, it was simply inconceivable for me; I was scarcely able to keep my feet in a carriage in ordinary circumstances.

After a few trial and error attempts which almost ended in catastrophe, I finally found a route. I would take the metro opposite my place to where the number 74 bus started on Rue de Rivoli – then, after brandishing my disabled card to get a priority seat next to the driver, I would head off to do battle with the traffic jams for an hour and a half. When I arrived, I would get off as best I could at Porte de Clichy, trying not to fall over. Then I would hobble painfully through the 300 metres of hazards posed by the horrendous building site that separated me from the courts. I would arrive sweating and exhausted. In the evening, when the traffic had calmed down, I would take an Uber home, completely wiped out. I couldn't help my daughter with her homework anymore; fortunately Hildegarde's mother was there to pick her up from school and watch her, otherwise I don't know what I would have done.

I kept that up for a fortnight, through to the third installation phase, all the while clenching my teeth and suffering snide remarks because I regularly arrived late no matter what time I left home, and then one morning I cracked and took the metro, telling myself that the packed crowd would keep me upright without me having to cling onto my crutches. But when the door opened at the Porte de Clichy station, I was swept up so violently in the surge of people getting off that one of my legs with its orthosis slipped into the gap between the carriage and the platform, and if somebody hadn't had the presence of mind to pull the alarm, it would have been ripped off when the train departed.

I arrived at work trembling and started to cry uncontrollably. Hildegarde called my boss, who put me on sick leave for a month.

That's when I went to my father's birthday and, well, the rest you know.

The Iroise Sea
15 July 1870

Jules could not believe he had made it to his destination after such a terrifying crossing.

The previous night, the doorman of his hotel had unearthed a lugger that had docked in Brest to deliver crustaceans and load up on barrels of alcohol while waiting for the tide to come in. Delighted to be making the trip, Jules boarded at sunrise in excellent humour. The crossing promised to be magnificent; a mirror-flat sea and a gentle wind indicated a seamless trip and a late-morning arrival.

Once they had left the harbour and their course was set for the island, he attempted to make conversation with the crew, but very quickly, upon sighting the numerous rocks punctuating their route he realised that any failure to open their mouth was due to their watchful scrutiny of the water's surface as they navigated a path through the reefs revealed by the ebb and flow of the swell.

He had been warned that he was heading into shipwreck territory, but he took that as mere tourist puffery; a low-cost way of giving them a taste of adventure. Unfortunately, they had not been lying. It appeared he had embarked on an egg with a fragile shell just waiting to be smashed on the multitude of rocks breaching the water's surface. So he remained silent and let himself be enthralled by the grandeur of the landscape, which was as beautiful as it was inhospitable.

The vessel plied its way along the island's coast, its cliffs looking as welcoming as a herd of pachyderms about to charge, then it rounded the point to arrive in a harbour protected from winds and currents, where it dropped anchor. The crew lowered a rowboat into the water and standing upright, surrounded by barrels of alcohol, Jules once again made landfall.

After disembarking onto a deserted jetty, he headed off on foot to the village centre. He did not encounter a living soul, except for a few very small, curious, gaunt-looking black sheep, half-heartedly jostling their way across his path.

Church bells were announcing the end of Mass.

The doors were flung open and, all of a sudden, the square that seconds earlier had been deserted was invaded by women.

Hundreds of them.

Women everywhere. Women like he had never seen before: tall, thin, their dark hair cut level with the nape of their neck, their faces etched by the sun. They all wore the same black outfit, like the women he had seen on Corsica, except that these women wore their skirts to just below their knee. As the more elderly among them scattered to the four corners of the island in endless black lines, the younger ones flocked around this moustachioed man with his flame-red hair who had just miraculously appeared in the centre of their village. They were all openly smiling at him, their gestures and glances imbued with the knowing experience of the most brazen prostitutes. Apart from a few old men and young children, there was not a single man to be seen. It was a garden of Eden populated entirely by beautiful, flirtatious, strong-smelling farmgirls, their hair ill-kempt under their little white bonnets.

It had been a rough crossing, but Jules de Brassac had landed in paradise.

Unable to believe his luck, he allowed himself to be led off by a flock of merry young women to a bar called Le Kastel, which already had a virile, guardhouse atmosphere. Mothers, young women and the elderly were all downing glasses of alcohol, cheerfully exchanging insults and curses from one table to another in an incomprehensible dialect. The matron behind the counter greeted him like a long-lost friend and served him a glass of some corrosive liquid that he had the unfortunate idea of tossing back in one go. She refilled it immediately, clapping him vigorously on the shoulder to encourage it down: 'Drink up, handsome traveller, in these parts you can't leave your glass full for long,' she said to him in French.

All eyes in the place were fixed upon him.

The older women were nudging the younger ones with their elbows, bawling in their drunken, rasping voices ... *Krog pa gavi* ... *Krog pa gavi* ... Whereupon everybody howled with laughter, their faces buried in their glasses.

He had barely finished his second pot when an enormous man who looked to have stepped straight out of some local legend, made a thunderous entrance. Jules recognised him as the local priest from the robes he was wearing. The man castigated Jules' young female companion in furious Breton dialect, grabbing Jules authoritatively to haul him from the bar and back to the presbytery.

'An unaccompanied man should not be loitering here, it's not suitable,' he growled darkly.

'What a place, upon my word! Never have I seen the likes of such a place and God knows I've seen my fair share,' said Jules, a radiant smile on his lips. 'They're all saying the same thing ... *Krogpagavi* ... Is that the name they've given me?'

'*Krog pa gavi, ne vezo ket peh a ini: if you find one, sink your hooks in, there won't be enough to go around!* As you will have worked out, men are a rare commodity in these parts. They inspire covetousness and are the cause of many a scrap among the women.' He was silent, pointedly holding the gaze of his interlocutor. 'We wouldn't want that now, would we?'

As they made their way, chatting, back through the village, a throng of girls escorted them at a respectful distance, beyond the reach of the priest's sweeping gestures, which sought to shoo them away as you would flies. They accompanied the two men to the steps of the presbytery and waited for Jules outside.

With heavy gestures and hands like great paws, the man of the cloth removed his chasuble and stole, folding them carefully while his visitor set out the reasons for his presence on the island.

'You have been misinformed, Monsieur: there are no men here. No sooner have they left childhood behind than they join the Navy or Merchant Marine, to return only twice a year.'

'Rest assured, I am not some broker engaging in horse-trading. I have been sent directly by my family-in-law. Very respectable people who are seeking a substitute for their young son, who drew a bad number in the ballot.'

'How much is the father prepared to offer?'

'Casimir de Rigny is prepared to pay 8000 francs. Half upon signature before a notary in Brest, and the balance a year and a day after the date of enlistment into the corps. I shall bear the cost of the journey by train to Paris, as well as tobacco and kit, plus 50 francs for your poor box.'

'I would prefer 100!'

'I'll go to 100 if you find me a handsome specimen.'

'A handsome specimen, a handsome specimen ... Perhaps I can indeed find you a handsome one, yes ... Let me see. When do you leave?'

'Tomorrow morning would be perfect. Today is the 14th. It is imperative I be back in Paris by the morning of the 17th, with or without a man.'

'Oh no, that is not how things work around here! Either you reboard the lugger at high tide, or you remain here with us for a week, perhaps more if the weather is bad.'

'Ah,' said Jules, with some regret, having already imagined himself in orgiastic scenes with all those beautiful farmgirls lining up outside his door. He sighed. 'I have undertaken to return prior to the sitting of my brother-in-law's recruitment board. I am thus obliged to leave.'

'I know a kelp farmer who has just lost his boat ... Perhaps he would agree to sell himself. I'll scrub him down for you before I show him to you.'

Then, the priest, drawing himself up to his full height, cut a path through the young women, literally batting them away with his hands to disperse them, and escorted Jules to the front door of a small inn located directly opposite the presbytery.

'I will be quick, but I ask you expressly not to leave this spot before I return.'

The room where he was supposed to wait for his man was furnished in astounding fashion. Every item the merchant seamen of that family had brought back from their travels was crammed into the space, not so much with a view as to what might look well together, but simply as to what might yet be squeezed in. A six-foot-tall Venetian mirror sat over the chimney, hobnobbing with two porcelain tea services and a ravishing collection of netsukes that one might have expected to find at the home of a shrewd *japoniste* from the Palais-Royal. When Jules expressed his astonishment to the priest, he replied wearily:

'*Chinoiseries*... They're all returning with *chinoiseries*... That, and palm trees. The gardens on the island are all full of depressing palm trees. Everybody wants their own. They don't acclimatise at all well to the wind and salty sea air, but nor do they necessarily die. They struggle on, season after season. And yet they keep bringing them back here to die. I was born on the Île Bourbon, you know, and the palm trees there are something else,' said the man of the cloth wistfully.

'What a curious damnation!' thought Jules, watching him head off. 'What could he have done, that poor fellow, to be exiled so far from home, in this gynaeceum encircled by water and battered by winds?'

He was served an excellent meal featuring lobster, and scarcely had two hours passed before the priest reappeared with a man who had clearly taken very particular care in his attire, so well-groomed and close-shaven was he, and looking quite exalted in his Sunday best.

Jules could not help but note, from the manner in which this former Indian Ocean local introduced the kelp farmer in his best light, the way he skilfully had him open his mouth to confirm the state of his teeth, and made him jiggle about, hopping from one foot to the other so the deftness of his limbs might be admired, that the priest was quite in his element when it came to the presentation of his human merchandise.

'Breval Botquelen, twenty-five years old. His boat has run aground and the family of the young woman with whom he's in love no longer wish to have him as a son-in-law because he is too poor. He has told me he is willing to serve in your brother-in-law's stead at the price you are offering.'

The poor devil, upon hearing his name, sketched a timid smile in an attempt to render himself more attractive to his purchaser.

'He looks to be in excellent health.'

Then, drawing closer, 'Glowing even.'

'You wanted him handsome; I've coated him in palm oil.'

'Good, I like him. I'll take him.'

The priest translated the terms of the transaction into the Breton language for Botquelen, who, rather absent-mindedly, approved, but he added a further term in his native language which appeared to be a determining factor for him.

'He would like it expressed in the notarised deed that you shall have drawn up in Brest that half the amount to be received upon signature be paid to Corentine Malgorn, the girl who asked him for his hand. He says to tell you that he is off to say his farewells to her and that he will join you when the boat is due to leave.'

'Did I hear correctly: *the girl who asked him for his hand*...'

The priest gave a resigned sigh.

'Yes indeed, they do that too!'

At around 5 o'clock in the evening, Jules was back on board the lugger, watching the island recede into the distance.

He imagined he was one of those explorers in the Jules Verne novels of which he was so fond. Those travellers you assumed must be mad when, upon returning home, they tried to recount all they had seen during their extravagant adventures.

An island where the women asked the men for their hand in marriage: who would have believed such a thing? He promised himself he would one day return to this land of plenty or at least would set down his adventures to sell to a few Parisian rags.

He was no longer afraid of running aground. He was in a lyrical mood in this grandiose setting, as those seasoned sailors guided him through the danger. He contemplated the handsome five-foot-six specimen he was bringing back to his family and congratulated himself on offering the army such a fine recruit. How fortunate they were to have the common people to carry on the ancient vigour of the French race, for if they had to rely on the bourgeoisie – where the only things growing anymore were feeble saplings such as his brother-in-law, Auguste – they were a long way from winning that confounded war against Prussia.

As for Breval, who had never set foot on the mainland, he could not begin to imagine what the world might be like; Paris or the moon ... He decided to curl up in a corner of the boat in his Sunday best, and let himself float away on the memory of the sweet warmth of Corentine's body, having just made love to her for the first time.

6

IT DIDN'T TAKE ME LONG to find a much more plausible explanation than the one I had been offered as to the origin of my name. It started with a completely stupid question: if there was nothing in the official register of births, deaths and marriages as to when Auguste had died, even though he was twenty years old in 1869 – namely, one year prior to the declaration of war against Prussia – perhaps it was quite simply because he had gone to the front and there had met his end ... In those days, men didn't wear dog tags, and when they were killed and their bodies found, they would frisk them quickly to see if they had any papers on them that might identify them and then tipped them into a ditch with those from the opposite camp to avoid the spread of illness.

So, because I would have at least liked to know the history of the regiment in which he had been enlisted so I could imagine how his last hours had been spent, I began to dig around.

I didn't even have to budge from home because the military enlistment registers from Seine-et-Oise – seeing he was from Saint-Germain-en-Laye – along with army number records, are all available on the internet from 1867 onwards for any genealogy fans. And do you know what I found under the de Rigny name? I'll give you three guesses ...

Auguste – a tall, skinny thing measuring 1 metre 77, with blond hair, brown eyes, a straight nose, high forehead and oval face – had been selected in the ballot of 18 January 1870 and was enlisted in the 28th line infantry regiment on 18 July, that is, on the eve of France's declaration of war against Prussia. And then, in the space headed *Decision of the Board and Reasons*, below his personal information and physical description, there appeared the following note: *Replaced by Monsieur Breval Botquelen, born 14 August 1845, kelp farmer, pursuant to the notarised deed drawn up on 16 July 1870 before Maître Hippolyte Marie de Kersauzon de Pennendreff, notary in Brest.*

There it was! The missing piece of the puzzle!

Breval Botquelen.

A name from my part of the world, emerging from the depths of time like a piece of wood, swollen with water, that one day floats up from the deep.

Long ago, for my thesis, I had had reason to study Octave Mirbeau's novel *Sébastien Roch*, and I was immediately reminded of this extract:

> Today, I had to draw my name from the ballot, to draw my lot, as they say, and I was unlucky. My father has bought me a replacement. I shall forever see the face of that merchant of men, that trafficker in human flesh, as he and my father discussed the deal for my redemption in a little room in the town hall ... They haggled a long while, franc for franc, sou for sou, growing

animated, cursing one another, as if they were dealing with livestock, and not some man I did not know, and whom I love, some poor devil who will suffer for me, who will perhaps be killed for me, because he has no money. Twenty times I was at the point of halting this sickening, this torturous argument, and of shouting: 'I will go!' Cowardice held me back. In a flash, I envisaged the hideous existence of the barracks, the brutality of my superiors, the barbaric despotism of the discipline, the degradation of man reduced to the state of whipped beast. I left the room, ashamed of myself, leaving my father and the slave-trader to negotiate this abomination.

I wrote immediately to the notarial archives in Finistère to obtain a copy of that deed of sale dated 16 July 1870 referenced in the army records.

When I returned from Brittany, while still on sick leave, I wasn't content just to throw myself into my family history research, I also did something worthwhile.

Let me say this clearly and unequivocally: *I did something worthwhile!*

In order to hand in my occupational health and safety documents and give some instructions to my friend Hildegarde, so she could fill in for me during my absence, I went back to that damned new Palais de Justice. I took the chance to grab a few drug squad CD-ROMs, not wanting to laze about too much, as well as pick up the *Oilofina/de Rigny* file, which I now had access to without having to ask my friend, since the financial crime department's database had merged with ours. I had no plan. I just decided to do it out of curiosity, really. That evening, after putting Juliette to bed, I sat down on my bed with my computer on my lap. I inserted the disc into the drive with the primary thought of reading a good adventure tale before falling asleep.

At the start of 2013, cousin Philippe got wind of a stockpile of 30,000 tonnes of hydrocarbon originating from a failed crude oil refinement process. As it contained far too much sulphur, this *naphtha* – that's what this distillate is called – could not be sold on the market unless it was processed again. It was taking up tanks at an oil terminal in the United States and its owner wanted to get rid of it at rock-bottom price.

So the Oilofina boss thought to himself that with a bit of ingenuity and audacity, he could buy this defective naphtha and turn it into mediocre-quality diesel himself, which he would then on-sell to the Africans, making a pretty packet in the process. In Europe, fuel sold into the market is not allowed to exceed a certain limit of sulphur content in order to comply with environmental pollution regulations, but in Africa it's different. People drive around in wrecks running on diesel that exceeds the regulation limit by five hundred times, and the brokers call it *African-quality diesel*. Millions of people die every year from respiratory diseases caused by sulphur dioxide, but the rest of the world couldn't give a shit and brokers like de Rigny grease the governments' palms so the regulations, or rather the lack thereof, remain as they are.

The odyssey starts.

Three characters in this story: the cousin, of course, with his genetic nose for business. An obscure Russian ship's captain, globalisation's dogsbody, used to receiving his orders via satellite telephone without ever meeting his employers. And of course, Africa. Africa, which rhymes with moolah, corruption, scapegoat, impunity, coup d'état ... Complete walk in the park.

Philippe de Rigny is in the oil-broking business and not in refining, but that doesn't matter, because there's nothing a de Rigny doesn't know how to do.

So he decides to desulphurise his naphtha himself, using an age-old, polluting procedure – the merox process – which consists of washing it with caustic soda. You put the naphtha and the soda into an uncovered vat and after twenty-four hours a disgusting diesel floats to the surface while the sulphur, combined with the sodium and oxygen, falls to the bottom of the vat. This residual product is ultra-toxic and corrosive. It looks like thick black syrup and gives off a gas that has the stench of death: this is the mercaptan that everybody knows about because it's used to perfume our town gas so leaks can be detected. The cousin calculated that if he sweetened his 30,000 tonnes of low-cost naphtha on the cheap using the merox process and resold the diesel fuel he thus obtained to the Africans, he would be able to pocket 7 million dollars. And in order to make an even bigger profit margin, he decides to carry out the chemical reaction himself – where? – on the high seas, of course, right there on his tanker, in international waters, where nobody will come and give him any grief.

In order to do this, he charters a floating wreck from a scrapyard in Bangladesh and recruits a cheap crew, no member of which speaks the same language nor asks any questions. The Russian captain's orders are to make his first port of call in Europe in order to take delivery of 50 cubic metres of liquid caustic soda, which he will declare is to be used to clean the tanks on the old freighter. The vessel will then head to Africa, but will stop for a while off Gibraltar, where several other boats will be waiting for it after returning from the United States, where they had gone to take delivery of the naphtha. And right there, on the high seas, ship to ship, is where the blending will take place, with the boats separated by old rotten fenders to prevent their hulls from colliding. At any moment, it could turn into an ecological catastrophe, but de Rigny doesn't give a damn; after all, these things happen, especially in international waters.

In order to monitor his unauthorised refining process, he has personally, at nearly seventy years of age, helicoptered out to the boat, carrying 8 kilograms of cobalt catalyst to set off the chemical reaction. The age at which he is schlepping around, suspended in the air, is an interesting detail worth mentioning in order to understand just how much joy he gets from watching his dough being generated right before his eyes. The mixture circulates from vat to vat and the 30,000 tonnes of naphtha slowly get washed, and the sulphur levels fall sufficiently to allow the production of very poor, *African-quality* diesel.

Once the operation is finished, the Russian takes off in his tanker again to go and deliver the diesel that de Rigny has just sold over the telephone to Togo and Nigeria. But once the hydrocarbon is unloaded from the ship, he still has to get rid of the ultra-toxic black sulphur syrup: the slop. The problem is that they don't want it in Lagos – the only port capable of retreating refining waste – because the oil terminal is run by a former Oilofina employee who evidently knows de Rigny too well to accept it. In Ghana, he's presented with a quote of 3 million euros, the same price as in Europe, which would ruin his margin. Nor can he tip his slop into the ocean, because having made the mistake of trying once or twice to have it retreated, he has thereby rendered his toxic waste traceable. If, in the unlikely event, Oilofina were to get caught in the process of the unauthorised cleaning-out of his tanks, that would be considered an unpardonable display of bad taste in the small world of petroleum.

Thank God, that still leaves him French Africa. And it's in this direction, where he has unwavering supporters, that de Rigny turns to rid himself of his filth.

Somebody – political acquaintances, people at the foreign office at Quai d'Orsay, we'll never know – *somebody* found him a fantastic Ivory Coast company specialising in cleaning the holds of ships, a company run by a completely moronic fall guy, whose shareholders are all ultra-corrupt dudes from customs and the port authority. After having paid off whoever was necessary, he signs a contract for the *African-style retreatment* of his waste for a ridiculous amount, with the fall guy not stopping for a single second to interrogate him about the nature of that waste. Thus, the businessman shifts his legal liability to the respectable fall guy and the slop is pumped off the ship in the direction of a flotilla of rusty tanker trucks that disperse to the four corners of the town. De Rigny, with the satisfaction that comes from a job well done, goes home, and the Russian heads off with an empty tanker back to the scrapyard.

Then, what was bound to happen, happens: the slop is poured out, as is, into the rubbish dumps of Abidjan. The black syrup burns several people to death, some of whom are children rummaging around in the scraps. As for the mercaptan, it seriously poisons more than one thousand locals and sets off a panic that increasingly resembles a civil war. But it's not de Rigny's fault; he has done nothing illegal. So, when Transparency International brings proceedings against him *in personam* and against his company Oilofina for the bribery of foreign public officials in order to try to repatriate the dispute surrounding this ecological disaster to France and thereby to avoid him settling by way of some baksheesh, cousin Philippe screams injustice and persecution.

The years roll past, the NGO evidently struggles to present proof of bribery and the matter which was brought in 2014 slides sluggishly towards dismissal. And because they have an accommodating memory in French Africa, de Rigny calmly resumes his petroleum business with Ivory Coast.

But a few months ago, out of nowhere, there's a bolt from the blue: our African friends have all of a sudden grown resentful. For some obscure reason, Oilofina has fallen into disgrace and the powers that be have had Philippe's son, Pierre-Alexandre, arrested on the tarmac where he was waiting for his private jet after signing agreements for his daddy in Abidjan. And given the number of his alarming letters addressed to the Quai d'Orsay, it didn't seem like he was having much fun in the Maca prison where he was incarcerated.

Far from distracting me or sending me off to sleep, reading that file sent me into a blind rage.

I found it unacceptable, first of all, that one might ostentatiously consider one section of humankind to be worthless simply because they live in a poor and corrupt country.

What outraged me still further was the scant regard shown for the ocean. To me, the sea is no minor matter. My entire childhood was steeped in it and, wherever I am, I feel suffused by it. The sound of the ocean, the incessant noise of the billions of pebbles rolling around on top of each other, the sound of the waves bashing against the seawall of the port: I can still hear it all in my sleep. Nobody ever thinks about protecting the sea and the animals that live in it from unscrupulous rotten-to-the core swine like de Rigny and his offspring. If nobody stops these people, they'll continue to appropriate what little still remains for the taking before it all disappears while penniless environmental crusaders desperately try in vain to save what can still be saved.

Finally, what revolted me most of all was my own frustration, my inability to understand the motivations driving these businessmen to destroy our children's future just to earn a bit more money, when they had stockpiled enough to support another four hundred generations. What goal were they pursuing by ruining the lives of those who have next to nothing by taking what little they still had? Were they doing it for laughs? To be able to tell themselves they were the best? For the drunken ecstasy prompted by the suffering and destruction?

Was this the situation Jesus was anticipating when he said, in a great moment of irony, for which he is not typically known: *For whoever has, to him more will be given, and he will have abundance: but whoever does not have, even what he has will be taken away from him*?

The response to all these questions was even more distressing than one might imagine: the de Rignys, while making ever more money, were not pursuing any particular objectives, the accumulation of wealth being for them just a process. Having made their fortune in the nineteenth century, the capitalist dynamic created a snowball effect. The more significant their total net worth, the more money they amassed when they took it for a whirl on the financial markets. And the few extravagances they shouted themselves with their enormous dividends – the yacht, the property in the what's-it-called islands built by the latest trendy architect, the clothes, the jewels, the paintings, and the god knows whatever else – were certainly not about to prevent them reinvesting it to make even more.

It was a phenomenon that had fed off itself for a century and a half and which, by its very nature, was going to continue to grow and grow until a little lame beetle came to insert herself inopportunely into its workings.

The final page of the file had been scanned two days earlier. It was an order by the Minister for Justice pardoning Pierre-Alexandre and providing for his release from the Maca prison the following week. I imagined the number of intermediaries that would have had to be mobilised, the sums of endowments promised, to secure such a *lettre de cachet*.

It seemed self-evident that it had to be stopped. I didn't even pause to consider. I stayed awake until morning, then, after dropping my daughter at school, I went to the former Palais de Justice building, which was almost deserted. So my IP couldn't be traced, I used an old terminal that was still connected in the part of the building normally occupied by investigating magistrates, and I simply flooded the social networks of African newspapers with that document, as well as the inboxes of victims' associations whose addresses I had found in the file.

Back then, I had never travelled outside France, but I had always heard my father and his Merchant Marine mates talking about the different ports where they had docked during their career, particularly those in Africa. They always used to say the same thing: it didn't matter where exactly they were, the atmosphere was such a tinderbox they never really felt safe.

A place could be perfectly calm, people quietly going about their business, and then all of a sudden, because of some rumbling coming from who knows where, crowds of angry rioters would appear in the streets brandishing all sorts of weapons. The fact that there's always an election on the horizon with candidates ready to spew their bile to the media merely served as a catalyst to the rebellion. When something like that happened, it was never a good thing to be white. You were always suspected to a greater or lesser degree of only being there to make money.

That was what happened in 2014 when Oilofina's slop made its pestilential appearance in the town's dumps. Quick as a flash, and with no warning, because the limits of what was intolerable had reached its peak, a hate-filled crowd had descended on the villas of both the Abidjan port manager and the environment minister, taken out their personal guards, pillaged everything they had been able to lay their hands on inside, and then set fire to what was left. The announcement on social media four years later of the date and time of arrival of a delegation comprising Philippe de Rigny, accompanied by a foreign office diplomat from the Quai d'Orsay and the Ivorian Minister for Justice, all three of them sent with great ceremony to Maca to release Pierre-Alexandre from prison, had the same incendiary effect.

Word of the impunity of those responsible for the environmental disaster ricocheted and spread, until a mob had gathered – and the prison was stormed.

The furious crowd went on the hunt for the de Rigny pair, making it all the way to the director's office, where father and son had tried to hide. Amid total chaos, the rioters dragged them into the street, while the guy from

Foreign Affairs locked himself in a cell and both the minister and the prison director did a bunk. The rioters set upon cousin Philippe and his offspring with sticks and stones, then sprayed their mutilated bodies with petrol and set them alight.

In Africa, this sort of lightning execution has a name: *instant justice.*

It looks like a storm and suddenly, once the tension has dissipated again, it stops dead in its tracks and everybody goes back to doing what they were doing. They're a little more analytical at the foreign office; they might mutter something along the lines of: 'In the globalised economy, it is possible to make money in any number of ways, provided one implements certain minimum procedures and applies discretion. De Rigny was unable to do this, which is regrettable.'

The lame beetle followed on Facebook Live the butterfly effect she had set off, doubtless being filmed by one of the recipients of her letter, then, after closing her computer screen, she went back to her research on Auguste de Rigny and his replacement, Breval Botquelen, satisfied to have accomplished something worthwhile.

'Come now, lads, please ... Could we not, just this once, have some pleasant, peaceful family time?' said Casimir, tapping the edge of his plate with his knife.

And he raised his glass.

'So ... Here's to Auguste!'

Ferdinand disregarded the toast as he continued to torment his brother.

'What was it you wanted to do, take him in your arms? Did you see him, father, with his replacement? You would have sworn he was some unmarried mother having her child wrenched from her to be handed over to welfare. You were grotesque!'

'To victory!' proffered Auguste's sister, Berthe, timidly, raising her glass in turn.

Auguste, for his part, had his head in his hands, scarcely able to contain his rage.

'Believe it or not, I would have appreciated having the time to thank him. When the recruitment board officers signed him up just now, he hadn't understood a single word of what he was being told. You and Jules could have given me just one day, one measly day – the day to which I was still entitled – and I might have telegraphed to have a Breton come to Saint-Germain ...'

'You would have *telegraphed to have a Breton come*,' repeated Ferdinand ironically, emphasising each separate syllable.

'Exactly so! A Breton. So his field orders might have been translated for him. But no, he had to be rushed off to the abattoir after twenty hours on the train like some common head of livestock.'

His brother-in-law, Jules, objected.

'An animal who travelled first class, I'd just like to emphasise. I had to keep him with me so nobody stole him from you.'

Ferdinand raised his eyes to the heavens.

'Brest to Paris first class for some beggar, now we've heard it all! And he had to be thanked on top of that? One does not thank somebody to whom one gives 11,000 francs!'

Casimir tried once again to declare a toast in honour of his son.

'To Auguste,' he said, with less conviction.

'To France!' cried Jules with all the heartfelt delight he was feeling from the 2000 francs he had filched with complete impunity from his family-in-law, not to mention the money spent on his orgies. 'In less than a week, your substitute will be in Berlin, and when his period of service is over he will return to his island, crowned in glory, to wed his beloved. You will even be able to visit him should you wish, so you can confirm he is happy back in his little paradise, with all his medals pinned to his striped sailor's jersey.'

Berthe tried to change the subject before it degenerated once more.

'Tell us, my darling ... What did you find there?'

'The lost innocence of an earlier age, my dear, that is what I found on that island. Simple people living off their crops and livestock, far from the ugly realities of our modern world. They lead a harsh life, true enough, but still they remain cheerful. And then there's the sea; it's such a thing of indescribable beauty in those parts.'

'How charming!'

'Indeed it is: quite charming. But it is an extremely perilous journey, for when the ocean swell reveals the rocks, it's as if they are calling you to them. Which is why the place has been able to preserve some perfectly astonishing traditions.'

Casimir was feeling so relieved at having wrested his young son from conscription that he had downed glass after glass and was feeling a little the worse for wear.

'Now this manhunt has ended in such happy circumstances, what is it you are proposing to do with your future, Auguste?' he enquired, light-heartedly.

'Two of my friends and I are considering teaching.'

'Teaching? So ... where would you do that? At the university?'

'Yes, at the people's university.'

'And what exactly is that, now?' asked Ferdinand, scathingly.

'A place where people are given the opportunity to transform their lived experience into political knowledge. Where they will be taught to act on their own behalf, sharing their experiences. A place where, simply put, we will create the possible. But above all else a secular place where they will not be perverted by some charlatan hope of a better life after death so they accept their current misery.

It was Condorcet who said: *Mankind is divided between those men who reason and those who believe.'*

This was too much for Ferdinand, whose face was twisting into a frightful rictus as he listened to his brother's enthusiastic explanations.

'*Create the possible* ... but my poor Auguste, there's simply no understanding a word you're talking about! Your problem is that you spend too long dreaming and you do nothing. Why don't you accompany me on one of our site visits? ... Do you have any notion what the most dreadful thing on a building site is? No? Well, allow me to tell you: it's a labourer who knows how to read! He gleans bits and pieces of knowledge that go to his head and lead him to believe he's entitled to all manner of things. And what's more, he infects the others. Aspirational types, vindictive and bitter sorts, dangerous people, that's what you get when you educate the masses. Thiers was right when he said: *An educated population is an ungovernable population.'*

After a brief moment of respite, old Casimir was once again overwhelmed by his old fears. 'How was it possible for a de Rigny to become a Red?' he wondered.

His youngest son, as well as having a weak constitution, must be suffering from some innate emotional disturbance. That had to be it. Some sort of organic stroke of misfortune suffered in his mother's womb. One more affliction to add to those he had caught as a child.

So, in a weary voice that betrayed his consternation, he said, 'But Auguste, the true grandeur of the people is to be found in their faith in God and in their ignorance.

In the spontaneous sacrifice of their existence for our well-being. To wish to put an end to that, to teach them how to read and how to think, would amount to sawing off the branch on which you are sitting. Why would you wish to devote your life to such a thing?'

7

ON THIS, THE 16TH DAY *of July, 1870, before Maître Hippolyte Marie de Kersauzon de Pennendreff, notary in Brest, Monsieur Breval Botquelen, kelp farmer, born on the 24th day of February, 1845, being 1 metre 68 centimetres tall with brown hair, grey eyes, a high forehead, large nose, straight legs, a round face, clear skin, a regular mouth, and a full set of teeth, … hereby agrees that he will be bound to serve in the armed forces as a replacement for Monsieur Auguste de Rigny of the commune of Saint-Germain-en-Laye, and shall continue to be so bound for the period for which the latter is required by law to serve. Monsieur Jules de Brassac, duly authorised for these purposes to act as agent for and on behalf of Monsieur Casimir de Rigny, father of the aforementioned Auguste de Rigny, shall accordingly lawfully pay the sum of 8000 francs pursuant to the following terms: 4000 francs in cash to be counted and paid over in the presence of the undersigned notary upon signature of this deed. The balance shall be paid one year and one day after the date of enlistment to the corps, during which time the substituted man is liable to the government for his replacement except in the event of death in the line of duty, whereupon the said sum shall immediately become payable. Said balance payment shall be made upon presentation of a certificate of service from the corps thirteen months after his admission. It is hereby noted, as requested by Monsieur Botquelen, that the sum received in these offices upon signature of this deed shall in turn be paid immediately to Mademoiselle Corentine Malgorn and a copy of the said deed provided to her.*

So there you have it.

My true forebear, the biological father of my grandfather, was definitely not Auguste de Rigny, but rather Breval Botquelen, a very handsome sample of cannon fodder, aged twenty-five years, standing 1 metre 68 centimetres tall, with clear skin and brown hair, a good set of teeth and impeccable legs. He had been in neither the Merchant Marine nor the Navy, nor was he even a fisherman, but a kelp farmer. A peasant of the sea. A pauper.

He followed a Parisian, Jules de Brassac, in order to be sold to a bourgeois man by the name of de Rigny, leaving a fiancée behind him, my great-grandmother Corentine. He no doubt took the decision to sell himself as a military substitute because the Malgorn family wanted none of him as a son-in-law, hence the falling out and ill will harboured for over a century.

He obviously knocked her up with a kid by way of farewell gift, because grandfather Renan Astyanax was born exactly nine months after the sale. As soon as her pregnancy became evident, Corentine must have been thrown out by her family. And she would have had no choice but to leave for the mainland in order to find her beloved so he would formally recognise the child – except that in the meantime the war of 1870 broke out and he disappeared off to the front. Thus, it was Auguste, the fellow whose father had purchased the man as his son's substitute, who legally recognised him, doubtless motivated by political idealism, but also and above all to make good the fact that a man had died in his stead.

Great-grandpa had cost the de Rigny family 8000 francs in 1870. I was no fool. The life of my forebear – some unknown kelp farmer – was not worth that price; that was just the amount his purchaser had the means to spend to avoid exposing his own son to the risk of being killed.

It is worth noting, as I discovered when researching the issue, that it was the only time in history – namely, on the eve of war in 1870 – that the poor have been worth so much. It was also in the nineteenth century, with the appearance of capitalism as we know it today, that philosophers, such as Engels and Marx in particular, started thinking about the concept of the reification of humans. Putting to one side the slaves of antiquity and the New World, who were not by law considered people, but rather chattels, the ability to set a price for a man was formalised with the enactment of the Gouvion-Saint-Cyr law in 1818 to regulate the practice of military substitution, which had been going on since 1797 but had resulted in numerous court cases and scandals.

These days there is still a monetary value to human life, but its calculation no longer corresponds so directly to the laws of supply and demand. Some fix it at one hundred and twenty times a country's per capita GDP. By this method of calculation, one French person is worth 5 million

US dollars, an American is worth 6.5 million and an Eritrean is worth 70,000: that is, more or less the cost of the 4WD that could potentially crush him in a rally. Other methods base it on two concepts: the potential usefulness of an individual and the amount of money a society is prepared to fork out in order to save a life. Using these calculations, one French person would be worth around 3 million, whereas an Eritrean, well, let's just say politely that they're invaluable. Once such a figure is fixed, nation-states can make trade-offs with respect to health-care expenditure that would not, therefore, involve rare conditions such as the one which my friend Hildegarde suffers from. Same thing can be said for public works. Behind every planning development – for example, an intersection or a new level crossing – behind every piece of infrastructure that might preserve a life, there is a necessary allocation of monetary value to that life.

In our case, it would appear that Auguste de Rigny saw his family attribute to him a future value that justified him agreeing to big money being paid to avoid the risk involved – and his father hadn't thrown his money away, because in purchasing my forebear, he probably succeeded in saving his son's life in the lamentable slaughter which the war of 1870 proved to be.

What was this ever-so-young man trying to say by waving at me from the past so I would not forget him? What had he done with his life? The guilt he might have felt because an unlikely kelp farmer had died in his place in no way diminished the impact of his actions, given that in 1870 you would not have burdened yourself with such details. Rather, for a poor man to die in a rich man's place would have been considered a fair manifestation of the cosmic order of things. Even if I couldn't ever really know him, I enjoyed wondering...

And, of course, it was fairly impressive to have in your hands your great-grandfather's deed of sale. Poor Botquelen! Dead like a dog on the side of a road. Lost to time, with nothing remaining of him but ill-defined traces. A description tossed off by a provincial notary and a little boy who didn't even bear his name, and here I was, the only person aware of the connection. While we're at it, about my grandfather, the old cripple perched on his barrel – there's another generation of cannon fodder, of organic reserves to which France has so generously helped itself. Fate has been peculiarly persistent in this family.

Paris
19 September 1870

It was bucketing down. Utterly exhausted, Clothilde was recovering with her feet up, having once again traversed the length and breadth of Paris to snaffle up the last remaining tins of Australian lamb, sardines or pâté from the grocery stores.

'Oh, some post. And here I was thinking we had been cut off from the rest of the world. Thank you, Rosalie.'

'Madame, I will need some money for tomorrow's dinner.'

Her employer pulled her purse from her sleeve, looking for a handful of coins.

'Oh no, Madame, I should only be able to buy one leek and an onion with that, and only if I went all the way to the markets at Les Halles to find them. And with Monsieur's greens and eggs, believe me, shopping is becoming a terrible headache.'

Auguste lifted his eyes from his paper. The Sorbonne was closed or, more precisely, had been transformed into barracks, so that was all he was doing now: reading the paper.

'I am not an imbecile, Rosalie! I know how to make do. Given the circumstances, I shall eat whatever is given me ... This war has forced me to drink down to the dregs, so a little more or less, really, given the current state of things —'

'There are soldiers dying for France as we sit here and speak of your diet, my dear nephew,' commented Clothilde, dryly.

'What can I say? There isn't a day that goes by that I don't think of him, my man from Brittany! I dream about him every night. And since we're in the process of confounding diet with patriotism, you should be aware that while you are out paying a visit to your suppliers of comestibles for your Tuesday gatherings, the men who are really doing something for Paris, the National Guard who are protecting our city walls, are doing so on an empty stomach because their wages do not permit them to buy any such victuals.'

Seeing that he had offended his aunt, he resumed in a more gentle tone.

'I'm only telling you this because I don't want your friends to come to your lunches simply to receive a plateful of food.'

Clothilde rummaged around in her purse.

'The Prussians shall not stop me from hosting my Tuesday gatherings . . . How much will a rabbit cost?'

'I saw some for 50 francs!' said Rosalie, sighing. She, too, was tired from this constant running around for a head of celery or a piece of meat. 'I've heard tell of some pigs being reared in an apartment. I've been promised a trotter, but it won't be immediately.'

'But how ghastly!' said Auguste, sighing. 'That's all we need in our building.'

'Well, actually, they're in the Blins' apartment.'

'But how ghastly!'

'Now you're irritating us with your *how ghastlys*! Fifty francs for a rabbit, but that's twenty times the normal price! How will those of less means cope?'

'You're taking an interest in the poor now; that's a silver lining to the siege!'

If the maid did not interrupt their squabbling, it could go on for hours.

'They're organising stoves for the town halls and they're talking of handing out ration cards for bread and meat, because they're starting to slaughter the livestock in the Bois de Boulogne, the Parc Monceau and the Luxembourg gardens; it would seem the animals there are all dead on their feet.'

'Well then, Rosalie, take everything I have in my purse and use your domestic ingenuity to prepare an appropriate meal. And if you find any more cans, buy them! No matter what they are! Buy everything you can find!'

Clothilde looked at Casimir's letter, turning it over and over.

'It dates from three days ago, this letter. I don't know why people are so despairing when the post has never been so swift. Here, read it to me. Tell me how my brother is faring.'

Auguste complied.

My dear son, and sister,
*   It is too late, we will not be coming to seek shelter with you in Paris. I'm using the last train to leave Saint-Germain tomorrow evening to send you this letter. It will be simpler*

for you to write to us, because it appears they will be implementing a postal system using zinc balls that will contain up to 700 letters and will follow the course of the Seine, like a bottle on the ocean. Or indeed hot air balloons. I have been informed that a postal hot air balloon will leave from Montmartre or La Villette at the end of every week. So do not leave us without news.

There have been various defensive measures taken around us here, with rampart defences constructed from trees and paving stones lifted from roadways in an attempt to slow the advance of the Prussians, but I hardly believe it will help, for we have neither an army nor cannons to defend the place. Nor are there any remaining gendarmes or forest wardens, and the town is as deserted as if stricken by the plague. The way things now stand, we have only ourselves to rely on.

Regardless, now that the frenzy surrounding our defence has once again subsided, there's a feverish waiting and it is unbearable. We have been bivouacking on the terrace of the house for a week now to make it easier to scan the horizon with the spyglass. We are at the point where we are hoping that when disaster strikes it will come as a relief. So there you are, I believe the moment has arrived. This morning, the brother of the maid from Chanteloup-les-Vignes stopped off at the house to announce that his village had been invaded by a battalion of Uhlans. They shall be upon us this evening if nobody thinks to blow up the bridge at Poissy, which is perfectly likely given the hopelessness of our army.

You are probably not aware of the fact that the town of Saint-Germain joined the Republic on the 11th. Auguste,

I am informing you that your brother has a seat on the new municipal council; he has taken advantage of the situation to enter politics.

The Prussians are continuing to advance and are not encountering any resistance, flooding the region with troops. They are extorting money in every town they come to, and it is in the pockets of the bourgeoisie that they come looking. Ferdinand says we have nothing to fear given our position and our privileged relationship with Monsieur Thiers, who is, so I'm told, very well regarded by these people. Nonetheless, we will be obliged to open our doors to them, for the officers are taking over all the comfortable mansion houses. It seems they are well bred and even Francophiles, which is something. So you mustn't take offence, Auguste, but I will have to offer your bedroom to a Prussian officer.

I know that you, yourselves, are preparing for the siege. The youngest of our neighbours, who left to seek refuge in Paris, have told their family about the flocks of sheep and herds of cows that have taken over the parks and gardens; about the hordes of soldiers on the boulevards, the villages along the Petite Ceinture railway that have been razed, the enormous earthworks and surrounding walls defended by cannons. They're solid, those walls, I saw them go up. They had a go at Thiers back when he had them built, but now, wouldn't you know it, everybody is most happy to have them. Nothing but good rubblestone and no debris to speak of: you wouldn't see such good work these days.

Apart from these somewhat peculiar details, I'm certain that nothing has changed in your parts, that Paris is

*just as carefree and the cafés just as full. Jules assures me
it would be impossible for the Prussians to invade because
there are two million of you and fewer than two hundred
thousand of them, as long as Bazaine and his army keep
them occupied somewhere. That said, they will lay siege
and reduce you to starvation, so I do entreat you: stock
up on supplies. Buy all the food and candles you are able
to find, for if we should believe our friend Pélissier, who
endured the siege of Sebastopol, those will be the first items
to go. You must also bring in some wood, for if the siege
lasts through until winter, I know you sufficiently well, my
dear Clothilde, to know that you would sooner freeze to
death than sacrifice so much as a stool.*

Auguste paused to observe his aunt's reaction.

'Ah, very funny! If we're cold, we shall go to the Folies
Bergère and dance. That's what we shall do!'

'The chief of police has closed all the theatres; a question
of propriety, it would appear —'

'What a nuisance!'

'— But since last week the theatres have been hosting
club meetings where people discuss the resistance. I've
already attended a few debates. There's much laughter,
hurling of insults, shouting and whistling, and people being
ejected ... People come to blows almost every evening. You
would find it very entertaining. There is also a whole host of
unsung geniuses who come to jabber on about their heroic
inventions to free Paris, like *Satan's Rocket* or *Prussic Fingers,* or other hare-brained ideas such as poisoning the
Seine or releasing the animals from the Jardin des Plantes

to attack the Prussians. Frankly, the Folies Bergère has become a lot more appealing.'

'Prussic Fingers, did you say?'

'A rubber sleeve featuring a little sack filled with prussic acid and a needle in the tip, which ladies would slip over their finger. The lady gives a coquettish wink to a Prussian, and should he approach, she pricks him with her finger and he falls down dead as a doornail.'

'Did they say where one might procure such a thing?'

'Come, come now, Aunt. It's a scam! For a start, why would prussic acid kill Prussians?'

'Oh, you're no fun! Continue reading, then.'

And he resumed.

In your last letter, Auguste, you told me how sorry you were not to have been accepted into the National Guard because you were not registered on the Parisian electoral rolls. I can only rejoice. First of all, we did not pay such an exaggerated price for your replacement so you could risk your life defending Paris. Secondly, your brother-in-law Jules told me that as those soldiers of fortune receive 1 franc 50 per day, everybody wants to sign up, including the ignorant, drunken brutes from the faubourgs, *lending them a very debatable moral worth. It seems they elect their own leaders and are demanding to be armed with chassepot rifles, to defend against the Prussians supposedly. It is no place for you, among such vile characters.*

In other news, young Perret has not returned from the front. We do not know where he is. We await word.

I believe that is everything for now. You are very much

in our thoughts. For our part, there is nothing for us to do but place ourselves in God's hands.

Wishing you good fortune, and vive la France!

'Nobody is telling me anything about my replacement —'

'Now we have the Republic, Paris will be like some feline gathering itself before it leaps. There'll be two hundred thousand of us and we'll join up with the armies in the provinces who are carrying on the fight.'

'And there's my brother, calmly advancing his pawns, perfectly happy to invoice for two-hundred-man-strong construction projects while only employing fifty labourers —'

'We shall eviscerate them!'

'With that obsequious lizard Thiers in charge, the family company will be able to line its pockets even more.'

'Yes, and what of it? Are we supposed to stop earning money for the pleasure of those who have none? Thiers' politics reflect those of the honest man who is keen for his business to flourish.'

'But, Aunt, you do realise! Ferdinand is going to be working for the occupier!'

'Well then, he'll just have to charge those pigs double!'

'One day I shall write a piece on this ability of the human mind to reconcile the irreconcilable in order to reduce one's inner conflicts. You will serve as my case study, Aunt, so expert are you in the field!'

'While you get around to writing that book of yours, let's go out. Why don't we dine at Brébant's while they still have something to serve us.'

'Wait for me downstairs, I'm just going to look for an evening paper.'

'Will you pick me up *La Mode Illustrée* ... So I can see a little how one is supposed to dress during a siege. Neoclassical, elliptical crinolines, flounces, crins ... Frankly, it's hard to keep up.'

Notwithstanding the rain, the streets were overflowing with people. It was as if the citizens of Paris, having been made prisoners in their own city, were living their lives exclusively on the boulevards.

Heading out, the young man came across a few neighbours seeking refuge under their umbrellas, all of them gathered around a worker in a smock coat perched high on a ladder, who was busy removing the Rue du 10 Décembre street sign. Among them, he recognised Monsieur Blin, the pig-breeder from the apartment on the fourth floor. Monsieur Blin was calling out to the worker.

'Eh, so what are they going to call our street now, then, my good man?'

'Rue du 4 Septembre, it seems,' answered a lady with a bird's nest chignon.

'*Vive la République!*' trumpeted Blin, cheerfully.

'It took him scarcely a week, that turncoat,' thought Auguste. To have listened to that amateur pork butcher prior to the defeat at Sedan and the surrender that followed, one would have thought it necessary to defend the Empire in hand-to-hand combat. On the 4th of September, the day the Republic was proclaimed – a fine celebration, as it happens, in radiant sunshine, with the whole of Paris in the streets and not a drop of blood spilt – he shut himself away in his apartment. And now here he was outside, a red carnation in his buttonhole, exclaiming in delight.

The worker, who was soaked and utterly indifferent to the commotion going on under the umbrellas, unveiled the new sign.

'*Vive la République!*' came the onlookers' chorus.

Impassively, he finished screwing on the rectangle of enamelled metal.

'Hey, you up there! Why aren't you saying anything?' asked Blin, his face upturned. 'Aren't you celebrating? Would you prefer the Emperor?'

'It's six of one and half-a-dozen of the other, and rotten they all are!' said the worker, calmly climbing down. 'I'm just putting up a new sign on an old shop, is all. That's not the future we're waiting for. Not at all.'

His last comment worked like a bucket of iced water tossed into the faces of those gathered.

'Riff-raff!' said Monsieur Blin.

'I know what you're all thinking, the lot of you ... That one day we're going to come for you with our women and kids, and we're going to eye your pretty apartment and say to ourselves: *Why, wouldn't we feel right at home in there!* Well, if you ask me, you should all feel guilty, good an' proper, even thinking such a thing.'

All of a sudden, the rain stopped and the sun came out.

The man went calmly on his way, taking his ladder with him, followed by the disconcerted looks of the crowd.

While some in Paris would head to the city's fortifications every day with their spyglasses, scanning the horizon for the Prussians' arrival, others, like Auguste, would rush to the news kiosks just as the latest editions of the newspapers hit the stands, trying to predict the future as they dissected the press.

In the evening, under the glow of the gaslights, debates on the footpath would often degenerate into fisticuffs, with passers-by forced to intervene to separate the combatants. It must be said that never before had History been the subject of such passionate conjecture, with each edition filled with its fair share of dramas, new developments and contradictions.

Hardly three weeks earlier, the newspapers had been reporting nothing but French victories, so people had fancied themselves having the upper hand. Windows were bedecked with bunting, people were singing *La Marseillaise*, and this went on until the end of August, when families started to receive the first letters from soldiers.

Saarbrücken, Weissenburg, Wörth, Reichshoffen ... the French army had suffered defeat after defeat. The illustrated journals had portrayed the carnage so vividly they had had to be hidden from young ladies' view. The left-wing press had immediately leapt in and published *in extenso* various letters recounting the generals' strategic foolishness and lack of preparation for war. People had stopped crying: *To Berlin!* They had removed the flags from their windows and started to recount tales of horror. There was talk of the pitiful state of military logistics, of dismantled regiments bivouacking in random locations, of the lack of preparedness in terms of munitions and other provisions. Of officers forced to go into schools to get their bearings, having thought about maps of the German territory they were to invade but not for a single moment about those of the French territory they had to cross. Of generals who had mistaken battlefields and others who had fired on their own camp. Every page bore the word *disaster*.

Auguste had seen the first soldiers returning from the front at the Gare de l'Est. Thin, exhausted, their uniforms saturated and looking as if they'd soaked up a year's worth of foul weather, and mortified with shame, they avoided the looks of passers-by so as not to have to recount the debacle they had witnessed. Whenever he came across one of them, he would enquire after the 28th line infantry regiment, the regiment with whom he was supposed to have served and in which his substitute had been enlisted. He had finally learnt that the corps had fought in the Battle of Gravelotte on 16 August, which saw an artillery assault the likes of which had never been witnessed in military memory: 1200 deaths, 4420 missing in action and 6700 wounded on the French side, with mass graves filled to overflowing with bodies.

Where, among those thousands of people from whom no word was getting through, could Botquelen be? Was he at least still alive? Not a day went by when he did not think about him, and now young Perret was missing too.

Dear God, how he detested war!

A deathly silence! As of yesterday, Paris is alone, ran the headlines of *Le Figaro*.

The young man flicked feverishly through the newspaper, unable to discover anything further about the siege. There had just been fighting at Châtillon, but most of the soldiers had fled ahead of the artillery assault. Believing themselves to be pursued by the Prussians, they had retreated to seek refuge within the city walls, sowing widespread panic and anxiety. Not only that, but all roads and railways had been cut, the outer districts of the city had emptied out, and all livestock from surrounding areas had been requisitioned. The city, like an enormous fortress, had raised its drawbridges and was holding its breath as it awaited the onslaught of the barbarians. From this point forwards, it would have to stew in its own juices.

He found his aunt's magazine, *La Mode Illustrée,* almost more interesting. Its front page featured the first battalion of female National Mobile Guards, *the Amazons of the Seine,* who would be seeking to defend the ramparts. A double spread was devoted to sketches detailing the uniform, comprising black pants with an orange stripe, shirt and black kepi with similar-coloured piping. Women of all ages and from any social circumstances were being urged to present themselves for recruitment at 36 Rue Turbigo *in order to share their disdain for death with their male comrades and thereby earn their emancipation and civic equality.*

The advertisement was so typically Parisian and hardly seemed serious, yet, he said to himself, it seemed everybody in this war had their place; everybody but him.

Even the Commune, already suffering from internal rivalries, didn't want him. The Forty-Eighters, the supporters of Blanqui, Delescluze and Pyat, spying an opportunity to make their grand return to politics, all of them had their sights set on the available positions, blocking access to the younger men. That said, there were some, like Vallès and Varlin, who had managed to get their way, but they all had at least ten years on Auguste and his peers. At one point they had been told, 'You too shall have your revolution in thirty years' time. In the meantime, watch on and leave this to us.'

8

AS MONTHS WENT BY, my curiosity about the de Rigny family did not wane. On the contrary, I would go so far as to say it developed into a recreational activity. I had followed the funeral of Philippe and Pierre-Alexandre on the internet with a certain degree of interest and I was a regular follower of the family's social media posts, so when, some months after *their tragic end,* I saw on Instagram that Adrienne would be exhibiting her works at the International Fine Art Photography Fair at the Grand Palais, I obviously resolved to go as soon as it opened so I could see what she looked like in the flesh.

I had never been to an event of that nature before, quite simply because I had never felt the need nor had I ever been sufficiently curious, and also because I thought I would feel out of place. Like having a coffee in a luxury hotel; even if I could afford the 15-euro coffee, it would never enter my head to do so. Because I'd be scared they would turn me away at the door for not being appropriately dressed ... Scared I would be made fun of because I don't get the social codes of that milieu ... In short, because I didn't want to stand out like a sore thumb. Much like in that passage from Zola's *L'Assommoir* where Gervaise's wedding guests decide to go and visit the Louvre because the weather's bad. The group of proles tip-toe through the halls of the museum, speaking in a whisper, and all the regular visitors give them scornful, condescending looks as if they were fairground freaks. People with unsightly bodies, undone by their labour and poor nutrition, causing offence in those refined environs by the mere act of wandering through them. The yellow vests of the nineteenth century.

All my prejudices were confirmed at the entrance, with the 40-euro ticket fee, which Hildegarde, Juliette and I were the only ones to pay, because everyone else was there by invitation.

As I consulted the prices in the catalogues of shots exhibited from galleries the world over, I thought to myself that here, finally, with the photograph as work of art, we had discovered a means of producing something of infinite value by virtue of the ability to reproduce as many copies of it as you want, for only the cost of the ink and paper. A money-making machine with neither central bank nor treasury. Much better than shares in a company, which necessarily involved whingeing employees at the end of the line. The holy grail of the capitalist dream. The trick was to rate the photo, and that was what all these cool types, beaming like so many spotlights directed at our failings and cheap clothes, had come to do in that great exhibition space.

'Why have we come to look at photos of poor people and old people and awful-looking places?' asked Juliette.

She was right: 80 per cent of the photos exhibited there had destitution as their subject matter. Not our own destitution: no dreadlocked punks with their dogs getting wasted in public squares, nor delusional schizophrenics being held upright by their filthy clothes. No vacant-looking immigrants left sitting on the median strip of the ring road, nor expressionless workers watching tyres burn. No bothersome controversial topics. Definitely not. No, just some pretty third-world deprivation. Some exotic squalor of the kind: *just look at the sublime patina poverty forms on the faces of these miserable people.*

I was certain that in my lists I would have the phone numbers of the contemporary photographers working with subject matter like that. They were the ones you'd find sniffing or shooting up the bad stuff in evil places so they could feel truly alive and tell themselves that things were really, really tough for them too.

I stopped in front of a monumental print that must have been 3 metres by 2 metres, displayed under Perspex cut into the shape of the African continent and depicting a waste dump of technological products covered in children dressed in rags hurling their anger at the blind lens of the camera fixed on them: 40,000 euros.

Dear God, I feel like gathering them all up in my arms, but there are so many of them...

'Well, well, hasn't the price of the poor gone up!' I said to myself, thinking back to my great-grandfather Botquelen and having a private chuckle.

'Who do you think would buy that?' I asked Hildegarde.

'I dunno, an IT company? A bank? I couldn't give a shit, it's sordid, I'd never put it up in my place. Oh, look over there! Dogs —'

And she was off with Juliette to a retrospective of a certain William Wegman, some guy who seemed to have built an entire career out of photographing two grey, rangy mutts. The artist was there at his stand, the poor bastard: *Could you guarantee that there is no animal abuse and exploitation involved in your pictures?*

'Go, Hildegarde!' I thought, 'Let's see you give him a serve.' I was already celebrating.

I took the chance while I was on my own to go to Adrienne de Rigny's stand just nearby.

They weren't really photos, what she was exhibiting. Choose your settings, press a button, all that was far too passé for her; the words *photographic truth is no longer to be found in the shot but in its appropriation* was written at the entrance to the stand just in case somebody (that would be me, seeing as there was nobody else) were to wonder why the artist was exhibiting photographs taken off YouTube. Except that we weren't talking about any old appropriations; they were images of her uncle and cousin being lynched, which had then been reproduced on a mount that looked like a metal road sign riddled with bullet holes. I discreetly went over to the catalogue to take a look at the price, and an even more discreet gallery assistant appeared out of nowhere to whisper into my ear that Adrienne's work had been acquired by the Pinault foundation.

'Must be a friend of the family,' I said to myself, 'Because otherwise … I don't get it! We're talking 15,000 euros.'

I took my time and pretended to examine each photo in detail so I could observe my cousin on the sly. Teetering on 20-centimetre high heels with an artfully dishevelled haircut, she had the sickly, bowlegged look of a forty-year-old woman who's starving herself, with the pit-of-the-stomach breath to match. She swept the space with a bored look – *what the fuck am I even doing here* – an e-cigarette in her mouth emitting a thick Tagada-brand strawberry-flavoured vapour, and her gaze passed over me as if I were a table, a chair or, better yet, a dustbin.

When Hildegarde and Juliette had had enough of torturing the dog photographer at his stand, they came looking for me at my cousin's.

'Did you see, Tata? That lady, she has the same name as us!'

'Oh, so she does!' confirmed Hildegarde. 'Come here, you, they're not pictures for a little girl like you.'

Like a duchess sizing up a cockroach, Adrienne grimaced in disgust as she looked at Juliette, then with a push detached herself from the wall, telling her gallerist in a weary tone that she was going to take a look around.

We spent a little more time looking at photos of poor people, then before we left I went to the bathroom: an enormous echoey room with a very high ceiling, tucked away at the back of the Grand Palais, with the obligatory black woman lurking in a corner, flanked by her cleaning cart.

While I was busy doing a wee, I heard an enormous gassy noise from the other end of the room, followed by a torrent of crap splashing into the basin.

'Yeah ... It's me, yeah ... No, not a soul ... Apart from two retard dykes and their moronic kid ... yeah, and it's my

stand they have to end up at … Stress … No, really, nobody!'
Sound of the door. Sound of the tap. No sound of the
flush.

'Yeah … I told you the comms guy was an idiot … Yeah,
I did tell you …'

Where do they teach you this sort of arrogance, which
signals to the whole world that you think you're better
than them? Is it genetic, or do they teach it in your second foreign-language class in one of those private schools
for people who are loaded? When I hear people talking
like that, I can't help thinking about that comeback from
de Funès to Montand in the film *La Folie des Grandeurs*:
'Don't ever apologise. Poor people apologise. If you're rich,
you're unpleasant, that's what you are!'

The strawberry-scented vape aroma, enhanced by the poi-
sonous odour of Adrienne de Rigny's diarrhoea, almost
made me retch as it reached me.

I pulled up my tights and headed over to the cubi-
cle which I'd heard her emerge from; indeed, she had not
flushed and the toilet bowl was splattered with a constella-
tion of shit all the way up to the lid.

Robot-like, the black woman swung into action with her
little trolley, heading towards the stench to do her job.

'Good, so are we off?' asked Hildegarde when I came out.

'I'm tired, I feel like sitting down for a moment and
watching the world go by.'

Just as I said that, a couple walked past sporting glacier

glasses and coats made from the fake fur of some other-worldly animal.

'Okay then, I'll leave you to it. Juliette, do you want to stay with Mum and count the lunatics, or do you feel like seeing a movie?'

Juliette started bouncing with joy and they left. I watched them for a while as they headed off, my heart overflowing with tenderness; my little girl knee-high to a grasshopper, with her 1-metre-93-centimetre-tall, spaghetti-limbed Tata Hildi in her trackies. Then my face twisted into a homicidal frown and I hobbled over to Adrienne's stand, hands gripping my crutches in rage. I planted myself in front of one of the panels that clearly showed the panic-stricken expression of Philippe de Rigny confronting his *instant justice* and felt a little calmer. The rioters had not yet started to attack him, but he knew that this time there was no getting out of it. His eyes, wide with terror, reflected not only the fury of all those about to set upon him, but the rage of every one of those subjects imprisoned in the images exhibited at the Grand Palais.

'Do you like it?' the gallery attendant was asking me.

'Yes, I like it a lot, that's why I came back. I can't get it out of my head, that photo. That's the one I'd like to buy, but I won't be able to with my credit card limit. I'll have to come by your gallery, but I'd love it if you could put it on hold for me. What would be the best way of doing this?'

'Well, you can pay me a deposit. What's the limit on your card?'

'500 euros.'

'Right.'

'I can pay you in cash or by cheque, but I'll have to come back tomorrow. Please, do you think you could put it aside for me?'

I had said it in a pleading voice, eyes wide, channelling a Stendhal-esque rapture.

'I'll go ask the artist.'

And the gallery assistant went off to whisper my request into my cousin's ear. She must have added something along the lines of *can you make an effort, please, go and talk to her, she really likes your work and she might be the only person who's going to buy anything*, because Adrienne came over to me with the sort of look that said, *gritting my teeth here, even though I might just crack them, but here we go.*

'So, it looks like you're keen on this shot?'

'Yes, hugely.'

'No problem, we can absolutely put it on hold for you until tomorrow.'

'You've managed to capture that exact moment where the milk's about to boil up and out of the pot. I find it so prophetic.'

'The pot. Yes. And what do you make of the gunshots to the mount? Do you like that?'

'Amazing! I've got a Facebook group that discusses photography that has lots of followers. I'd really like to introduce your work to them and, if you wouldn't mind, I'd love to share a little telephone interview. Would you be keen?'

I could tell by the displacement of air behind my back that the gallery assistant was gesticulating wildly to get her to agree. The digits of Adrienne's phone number emerge from her mouth, reluctantly, but they do emerge.

What happened next can be summarised in a few sentences.

I went home, compared her number against those of the drug users I have stored in the cloud and saw that it appeared in a dozen of the lists for cocaine and in four for MDMA. Adrienne was a regular user who bought decent amounts and had done so for years from lots of different dealers.

I also had in my database a short column comprising numbers of crack connoisseurs who only wanted to be supplied with pure cocaine so they could cut it themselves with bicarb and ammonia. I added Adrienne's number to these others and went across to my neighbours with my list. 'These people have a special order; if you hear about a pure cocaine delivery, they'll be up for it so they can do their cooking.' Mohamed graciously slipped me 300 euros for this latest list. I had a whinge, just for good form. 'What, you're kidding me, snow is worth three times that!' He made it 500, sighing.

The list must have done the rounds … A classy offer sent by SMS must have appeared on Adrienne's mobile at some point: *Sell CC KWliT XX, KWntiT limtd, order KWiK ++* … Because her dumbass arteries all of a sudden contracted and she died of a cardiac arrest.

Her friends posted *RIP Adrienne* in the comments on her last Instagram selfie.

With a sad emoji.

Paris
27 December 1870

The Grands Boulevards, usually so well lit, seemed to have narrowed in the half-darkness as a result of the gas rationing, taking on the appearance of medieval alleyways.

Auguste was holding his aunt Clothilde by the arm so she wouldn't fall on the patches of ice. They were both on their way to the Favié Club on Rue de Belleville.

'What was I thinking to agree to accompany you to such a place?'

'It gets you out of the freezing house where you are bored to death. And what's more, you're coming to admire your nephew, who will finally be speaking in public ... Well, I was asked to fill in because the clubs are losing all their speakers because of the cold, but it's a start.'

'Have you not had enough of this stupidity? Do you know what they remind me of, these Communards of yours? They're like animals who resist civilisation and who are just waiting for the right moment to come and knock down my door, steal my silver, piss in my sheets and burn down the building. They're envious, those people, I find them appalling.'

Auguste heaved a sigh.

'Still, the Commune stands for a little more than that, doesn't it? Civic equality between men and women, equality before the law for children born in or out of wedlock, secular, compulsory schooling that is free for all, including for little girls, the establishment of crèches so women are able to go to work … Really, Aunt, you declare yourself a feminist … does that not mean anything to you?'

'Contrary to what you might believe, I am not rooted in the past like your father. But you are young and you think you've invented everything when in fact the Commune is an old idea from 1848 and the same people are still running the show. Nobody has forgotten the progressive tax on private income and inheritance! All they need do now is add in the profits from our new public companies and the picture will be complete.'

'Well, the schools have to be financed somehow, don't they?'

'Indeed, but not with my money! I'm barely managing to keep my head above water as it is.'

'Money must flow freely in the veins of our society. And you, dear Aunt, are creating a clot!'

They both knew that to pursue the discussion further would only lead to argument. But that evening neither of them had the courage for it given their lack of sleep, the temperature that had plummeted to minus twelve degrees and the lack of food, so they fell silent.

Having come to the end of Boulevard Saint-Martin, they emerged onto the vast Place du Château-d'Eau, where a solitary gaslight flickered feebly, a spot of light amid the shadows. It was hard to believe that just four months earlier, that same square was being criss-crossed by carriages filled with people hurrying off in search of entertainment. They stood in respectful silence, much as you would at the bedside of a dying man; they felt profoundly angry at what the Prussians had done to their cherished city.

'Where are you with your collection for the cannons?' asked Auguste, gazing into the endless, black void.

'Well, it's not the people you'd expect who contribute. For example, the other day we went collecting in the 7th arrondissement. A very wealthy lady had just turned us away when her servant stopped me in the stairwell to ask if the poor were also able to donate. He went to fetch two francs for me. Women who are queuing at the stoves where soup is being handed out, who sometimes have to wait five hours in the cold, they run after us just to hand us a few cents.'

'And that surprises you?'

'I do not understand how one could not be patriotic at such a time, when the fortifications are holding in the east and we are still fighting.'

The hall of the Folies-Belleville where the Favié Club was meeting was plunged in semi-darkness and there was no heating. The blueish smoke from pipes added to the fug, shrouding the stage. There was a mixed and colourful crowd: many in National and Mobile Guard uniforms but also numerous working-class women with their infants asleep in their arms, as well as a few well-dressed bourgeois ladies; all were there to take advantage of the warmth generated by a collection of human bodies and to enjoy the distraction of the speakers.

When Auguste and his aunt entered the room, the topic of discussion was food supplies. The speaker on stage was talking about killing all domesticated animals, especially those horses used to draw mortuary carriages whose owners fed them bread, as well as companion animals.

'Let the rich carry their own dead,' cried one woman.

'Hear, hear!' agreed one section of the audience.

'I do not wish my dog to be eaten. I share my ration with him and that is entirely a matter for me,' added one well-to-do lady with a pug on her lap.

Laughter.

'Well, then, we shall hold off sacrificing that one, but keep a firm grip on him, that white sausage of yours, for we're all eyeing him off.'

Laughter.

'Next point: theft of wood from construction sites and the felling of ornamental trees.'

'We're cold!' came a shout from the hall.

'What people are doing now with all the wood? ... We should have done it a long time ago with the shop windows of grocers and butchers in the rich neighbourhoods. Let's at least strip the furniture from the mansions whose owners have left,' suggested one man. 'That will give us something to burn.'

Auguste leapt onto the stage and took over from the previous speaker, never taking his eyes off his audience.

'No, no, no. Envy will serve only to consolidate the enemy's strength, proving he is correct in his choice of society! The papers are telling us we have twenty-odd days of supplies left. We need to allow ourselves ten to replenish our provisions if we want to go out en masse to attack the Prussians. If we have not established the Commune within the next few days, if we have not pushed out this government of traitors who have sought only to negotiate a capitulation since the outbreak of war, then all the deprivations we have suffered will have been for naught.'

A member of the National Guard stood up, brandishing a menu.

'Look what I found! Elephant consommé, truffled antelope kidney, roast camel *à l'anglaise*, kangaroo stew . . . it's the Christmas Eve menu from Restaurant Brébant. That's why they closed the Jardin des Plantes! Because they sold off the exotic animals at outrageous prices to the restaurateurs of the Palais-Royal so the wealthy could gorge themselves while we fed on the tough flesh of old nags.'

Shouts. Nobody was paying attention to Auguste anymore.

'I'm fed up with cooking rat,' cried one woman.

'Try cat! It's not bad,' said another.

'No, kangaroo stew,' said a third.

Laughter.

The young man remained unperturbed and continued in a voice that he hoped was exhortatory.

'Citizens, men and women of the Commune . . . today we stand at the one hundredth day of the siege. If you do not seize this, our last chance to unseat this government, when the war is over, we shall be staring darkness in the face for dozens of years to come . . .'

But his words were swallowed by the brouhaha of the crowd.

'They found 1500 hams in an apartment building on the Montagne Sainte-Geneviève which copped a shell . . .'

'The hams . . . where did they end up?'

'Let's search the cellars!'

The sound of explosions cut short the interjections and in a single movement, everybody in the club rushed outside to scan the horizon, trying to work out the origin of the cannon fire.

In the east, the sky was streaked with light and pinpoints of fire.

'In this fog, it looks like the aurora borealis,' said the bourgeois woman with the pug.

'Here we go, they're bombarding us, the bastards,' said a member of the Mobile Guard.

Then the members of the Favié Club headed for home, disappearing in little clusters, one after the other, into the dark maw of the unlit streets.

Auguste, for his part, remained rooted to the spot, staring at his feet.

'The political thinking of these people extends no further than the contents of their plates. Nobody listened to me!'

'I'm hungry too. Shall we be off?' answered Clothilde.

9

MY MICRO-APARTMENT WAS just next to Boulevard de Sébastopol, so I had box seats for the protests that rolled past week after week. Notwithstanding the ever-changing roll call of participants – youth for climate, hospital staff, teachers, retirees, undocumented immigrants, students – all I saw was the same feeling of distress at being faced with the approaching end of the world. It won't happen like it does in Hollywood, you know, with Noah's Ark and a sea that'll swallow everything up one Monday morning. No. We were already there and this was how it was going to play out … with a gradual collapse of society's basic needs: housing, food, movement, heating, education, health, all of which were increasingly difficult to access for ever-larger numbers of people. It would start with social chaos, then an authoritarian regime voted in by the people to maintain law and order.

You need only have read Balzac, Zola or Maupassant to feel in your bones that the way the twenty-first century was starting out was very similar to the nineteenth. Of course, there was the progressive disappearance of public services, but not just that. After a twentieth century that had seen two wars and had glorified both qualifications and the entrepreneurial spirit, the share of a person's available means that was attributable to work-related income had gradually shrunk to exactly the same levels as those seen at the time of my forebear, Auguste. People were once again finding themselves waiting for Mummy and Daddy's money so they could afford to buy themselves a place to live or pay for their children's studies and support them moving out. And this trend would only increase with the end of growth – unavoidable in this depleted world – as we've known it since the Industrial Revolution. In other words: anybody with only their work to rely on, and no hope of inheritance, was asking themselves how the hell they could strike it rich when each year a more significant share of what they were earning was being swallowed up by everyday expenses and the little they managed to set aside was barely enough to cover inflation. It was becoming super-trendy to read Balzac's *Le Père Goriot*, with its priceless advice offered by Vautrin to Rastignac about climbing the social ladder, while the notion of the world as meritocracy was looking utterly uncool.

I was in a hurry to cross the boulevard to get to the Palais de Justice, where Hildegarde's case was being heard, but today's protest march was particularly endless. It was as if they had all agreed to stuff me around in a convergence of struggles based on a central idea that more or less sounded like *we want to be able to buy things too*. All you could say was that the claim really was the complete opposite of the sort of hostile proposition you'd expect to be aimed at the society against which all these people were railing; they could do nothing but voice their frustration, their discontent. It was such a pointless complaint when right next door, that very day, something truly serious was going down which really should have had them all gathering outside the gates of the Palais de Justice and getting ready to storm the place. Hildegarde, the sweetest, most inoffensive woman on the planet, was preparing to be sentenced by the Court of Appeal for having gained entry to an abattoir, where she had set up cameras in order to film the horrific manner in which the animals were slaughtered. And it was the second time she had done so.

After reading the charges, the chief justice noted that my friend was known –unfavourably – to the General Directorate for Internal Security for belonging to the vegan scene. So, the first thing I discovered was that there was such a thing as a *vegan scene* and that it was sufficiently threatening to warrant the payment of cops to keep my friend under surveillance and to regularly update her little file. And the other thing was that apparently the use of public opprobrium to stop animals from being carved up alive while suffering indescribable pain in order to fill tray-loads of meat which will for the most part end up being thrown away, all the while lining the pockets of an industry responsible for one of the principle causes of global warming, was considered a threat to public order ...

I mentally filed away the image of Hildegarde standing before those three judges, hands clasped behind her interminable back, head bowed to receive her punishment, right next to the image of the little girl stuffed into the backpack of that arsehole father of hers, and the one of the passenger who was incinerated on the day of my accident, and the one of the first jumper my daughter knitted, which she insisted on continuing to wear, and the image of the disabled people lacking hands laughing at the prawns they were supposed to shell. A collection of rare mental images that have shaped who I am and have made my life something a little more than a succession of Instagram posts.

She went from a four-month suspended sentence at first instance to an eight-month sentence with no remission on appeal, and as a result of her sentence being added to her police file she would lose her accreditation to work at the Department of Justice. She was being punished by removing her ability to earn a living. They were obliterating her.

It was when I emerged from that hearing (and not before, contrary to what one might think), with this distressing image permanently seared into my mind, that I started to think about the de Rignys' money and how we could put it to good use.

Were I to inherit that fortune, I was already considering that not a single cent would end up in the coffers of a state that was so obtuse, a state whose leaders, no matter who they were, would always use it for the short-term gratification of the masses in order to be re-elected and would never put forward an alternative model of society.

Frankly, it wasn't difficult to be an anarchist. If ever I needed further prompting, all I had to do was conjure up an image of the French government featuring the mug of the meat industry union's representative or that of the National Federation of Farmers' Unions, both of whom had been parties to the proceedings brought against my dear

Hildegarde, and that was all it took. And seeing as patrimony and capital were making a big comeback in the context of everyone's prospects, I told myself I really should move with the times.

Saint-Germain-en-Laye, Paris, Versailles
1 January 1871

Peace reigned in Saint-Germain-en-Laye, a Prussian-held town of 57,000 inhabitants, 17,000 of whom were French.

Once the brutality of the initial days had subsided, cordial relations were established between the residents of Saint-Germain and their occupiers. Whereas the homes of other families had been filled to bursting with soldiers, the de Rignys had received only Colonel von Gibintz and his aide-de-camp, whom they had installed in Auguste's room and in the garden shed respectively.

Wilhelm von Gibintz had nothing but positive attributes: he played the piano, quoted Victor Hugo with a delightful Teutonic accent, took every opportunity to apologise for occupying France, mourned his homeland where he was keen to return and where his beloved Gerda awaited him, bemoaned the obstinacy of the Parisians who were preventing him from doing so, and accompanied Jules on his jaunts to the numerous brothels that had sprouted like mushrooms in this town that was now no more than a garrison.

On this, the first evening of the year, with the women having hurriedly retreated to their bedchambers after supper so they might bury themselves in one of those dreadful, immodest novels of which they were so terribly fond, his son-in-law Jules and von Gibintz having taken themselves off for some revelling, and Ferdinand busy with his own affairs, Casimir gazed into the fire and reflected on the times in which they were living.

He had witnessed the Empire, the Restoration, the July Monarchy, the Second Republic, yet another empire and republic, and now this ... But for the first time, he had the feeling that regardless of what transpired, all that he had loved in his life had been irreparably lost. When the war finished, the world would embark upon a resolutely republican era in which nobody would continue to abide by the social hierarchy conceived of by the Lord in his wisdom. An era where uncertainty, chicanery and poor taste would reign supreme. Sighing, he told himself that such a world was truly not one for a peace-loving old man such as himself.

He gave another sigh. He, too, was tired of being French.

Absentmindedly, he picked up the *Allgemeine Zeitung*, which von Gibintz had left lying on the small pedestal table next to his armchair. There on the front page of the paper, in large gothic typeface, was the headline: *Was essen Sie denn?*[1], but as Casimir couldn't understand German, he put it back down.

*

'The Prussians must really be wondering what we're still finding to eat ... Well then, Rosalie, what will it be this evening?'

'A *gibelotte*!'

'Ah, very fine! A *gibelotte* made with what?'

---

1 So what are they eating?

'That is what's so wonderful about a *gibelotte* ... the white wine hides the taste of everything. I was assured it was dog's brains, but I think I've been had.'

'And these little round grey slices?'

'Oh that – they come from a batch of tins sold by a peddler from time to time on Rue de Rivoli ... He was unpacking them on the footpath just as I happened to be passing by. I managed to snaffle four of them. It spreads quite easily, but you'll notice the bread has a taste of sawdust today.'

Auguste pulled from his mouth a sort of thread that bore a very strong resemblance to mouse tail. He grimaced, but said nothing.

'In any event, one is left dissatisfied no matter what one eats. Thank you, Rosalie. Here, something to celebrate the first day of the year ...'

And his aunt pulled from her bag a little makeshift parcel, knotted in a handkerchief.

The maid unwrapped the cloth to find a large tin of preserved beef.

'Oh, Madame!'

Clothilde, who was dining in her overcoat due to the cold, covered her face with the two sides of her collar to hide a desperate urge to weep.

'I cannot afford to offer you money, for the way things are going I don't know how much longer I shall be able to keep all three of us. I shall make it up next year, if we are not all dead. In the meantime, how are you faring up there?'

'We are all sleeping in the room with the fireplace, Madame, and a friend has brought us some wood taken from public benches so we might heat the place.'

'By the way, did you hear those abominable screams yesterday evening?'

'It was the Blins butchering their pig. I'm still waiting for my trotter ... Methinks I'll be waiting for some time to come!'

The sound of cannon fire made them prick up their ears.

'Fear not! They'll never target the Grands Boulevards. If they did, wherever would they go for entertainment when they invade!'

Whereupon Clothilde scanned the room. 'Auguste, that pedestal table over there, it reminds me too much of the dreadful bore who gave it to me. Do burn it, will you, so we might start the year a little better than we finished the previous one.'

*

Ferdinand, for his part, was not quite living by the same calendar as the other members of his family.

There had been a before and after the arrival of the Prussians and there would be a before and after their departure. Thus, in *Prussian time*, he did not have a minute to lose and he was busy dashing from one construction site to another.

He had adopted the following syllogism: Saint-Germain-en-Laye and Versailles were two Prussian towns under Prussian administration being run by a Prussian administrator, which meant the public authorities were Prussian. The de Rigny businesses had always been engaged by the public authorities. Therefore, the company would work for the Prussians. And being the businessman he was, he saw only advantages to this reasoning, for the good thing about the occupying forces was evidently his ability to overcharge for everything, and to do so with complete impunity, since it was those who were being occupied who would foot the bill.

This collaboration with the Prussian authorities consisted of repairing the bridges and railways to allow their troops to continue on to Paris, as well as the forts to allow them to fire at will on the Parisians, but that was really not the point, because in fact business was so good that in barely four months he had already overseen what he hoped was just the first of a long list of capital increases in the life of his marvellous public company.

War and public works: what a splendid union!

With Thiers at Versailles to negotiate the armistice, Ferdinand had headed there to be in the box seat to witness the sketching out of his future. That which war destroys is always rebuilt, that was the rule. With a bit of luck, there would be vengeance, and another war, and then another: it was endless! At dinner on New Year's Eve he had overheard the following snatches of conversation from the government official sitting directly opposite him as he replied to his neighbour, who was troubled by the likely loss of Alsace and Lorraine: *At some point we will take back the provinces. It's the money we'll never recover.*

'It is the start of a formidable year indeed!' thought Ferdinand. He could viscerally feel himself amassing the fortune he would make from all this muck, and what a delicious feeling it was.

10

MY RESEARCH INTO MY FAMILY had foundered because I didn't know how Auguste had met his end. As for my collection of documents on the nine months between the sale of my great-grandfather and the birth of his son, I had to make allowances for source credibility, seeing as the available texts obviously emanated solely from educated people offering up a vision of the world which corresponded to their own bourgeois life experience. The others were, for the most part, illiterate.

Of course, there was Jules de Goncourt, with his excellent *Journal*. It was funny, sparkling, but horribly disdainful towards the *populace*, as he liked to call half of Paris. The other writers, your Maxime Du Camp, Alexandre Dumas the younger, Catulle Mendès, Leconte de Lisle, Henry Bauër, and even Zola with his *Débâcle*, as well as literary observers like Edmond Bossaut, Gustave de Molinari or Juliette Adam – the predecessors of bloggers – who described the siege as they walked the town, all managed to hint through their writing at the civilising nature of their way of life, often despite themselves. Had they had to burden their minds with concerns as unexciting as their livelihood, had they not had servants to look after their laundry, their housekeeping, their meals and their horses, it would have been impossible for them to create such beautiful works, to have such lofty thoughts or simply, like those few young bourgeois types led astray by the communalist adventure, to feed the revolutionary shitshow with their beautiful ideas. It seemed entirely normal to them to belong to a minority who were thinking on behalf of everybody else and not a single one of them could have imagined it any other way.

The only text emerging from the batch I had found was the diary of a gloomy nurse, one Victorine B, published in an even gloomier Swiss anarchist volume: *The Walking Dead – One Woman's Memoirs*. It had neither the style nor humour of the more recognised authors, nor the purely informative tone of Louise Michel. It had been written by a simple woman who was not seeking to impress, but rather to describe the siege as she personally had experienced it.

In answer to Jules de Goncourt's account in his *Journal* of his exhausting hunt across Paris for tins of boiled mutton and beef, she wrote:

To see the wealthy of Paris reduced to eating basic preserves, what irony ... Such dreadful times. The poor were not standing awestruck outside the shops, they had neither the time nor the means. While you, Sirs, conversed at Brébant's, Jacques Everyman was off to the ramparts, often on an empty stomach ... And if, by some misfortune, he had drunk a glass of doctored wine, feeling cold and hungry, and was a little merrier than usual as a result, he was called a drunkard.

This short paragraph both upset and alarmed me because there was the proof – self-evident – that nothing had changed one iota in the last one hundred and fifty years. Social groups continued to despise one another when the greatest challenge in the history of humanity was right there in front of us, namely that a share of the world's wealth no longer be used to make people richer, but rather to correct the harm to the environment caused by their actions so as to stop the situation getting worse.

When I shared my thoughts with Hildegarde, she replied very serenely that for 3 million years humans had cooperated in times of stress, regardless of their social status, and that quite on the contrary everything would work out very well. All you had to do was look at how people had behaved during times of great catastrophe: self-organisation, orderliness, mutual assistance and altruism always came to the fore, regardless of social background. Well, yes, that's true, but to get to that point, things had to be really very bad indeed.

How I loved her, that Hildegarde.

Hildegarde and her electronic ankle tag.

Since misfortunes never just happen as a one-off, I got a call from Granny Soize one evening: my father had not returned from his outing at sea. As I hung up, I said to myself, 'Well then, there we go, it's happened!'

It's often how they finish up, the old sailors on the island. One morning, despite the swell, they go out fishing and because they're stiff with arthritis they topple overboard as they're bringing up their pots. They no longer have the strength to haul themselves from the water to reach their boat's step ladder, they exhaust themselves and die of hypothermia. We all know they do it deliberately, even if we never talk about it among ourselves. They know that that's how it'll end one day, because they go out in any conditions with no telephone, no VFI digital navigation system, in unseaworthy vessels, but they don't give a toss: anything rather than dying on shore in a hospital bed.

I told Juliette the news. 'Grandpa has disappeared at sea and I don't think they're going to find him.' She asked me if I was sad. I replied no.

'You see, at some point birds get old and they die. So you would think you'd find lots of them on the ground or would even be hit on the head by one every now and again, but no. That never happens. Where do you think they go, all those old birds from the sky?'

She looked at me.

'I dunno.'

'Nobody knows! It's one of nature's mysteries. It's the same for old sailors like Grandpa. One day the sea just swallows them up the way the sky swallows up the birds.'

'Mum, you don't have to invent dumb stories for me. I'm not sad. Grandpa never gave a shit about me.'

'We don't say *shit*.' I was so gobsmacked by the accuracy of her remark it was all I could come up with.

Once again, I set off for the island, just to show my face, because frankly there was nothing I could do there to be useful. The national rescue helicopter searched for him for several days, then we waited for the sea to reject him. In vain.

No church service, because he didn't believe in God. Just a notice in the two papers, *Ouest-France* and

Le Télégramme, and most important of all a round spent sitting passively and listening to his mates at the Kastel rattle on about *how he was such a great fellow.* The gendarmes gave me piles of documents to fill out for the legal process of acknowledgement of death reserved for those circumstances where there is no body, but I left them all sitting on the corner of a table. It was the only way I could think to honour his memory: not to bother with anything administrative, and to tell myself that it would take care of itself. Which it did.

Still, it was a long week I spent waiting for a boat to take me back. I scanned the horizon from the port jetty, at precisely the place where the women of the island had stood for centuries scanning for a son, a husband, a brother or a father who wouldn't be returning. In my case, it wasn't an anxious wait, but rather a peaceful moment of introspection. The sky was low and the weather was fine. Everything was calm and soft around the edges. A bit like if you're sniffing ether or contemplating some great, empty space trying vaguely to remember what might have been there before.

After my escape to Paris at the age of thirteen, when my father lost it completely and gave me such a beating that if somebody hadn't stopped him he would have killed me, all of a sudden I ceased to exist for him. Never a single question about what I was doing or where I was going, nothing. We ate in deathly silence and as soon as the meal was over he unfolded his copy of *Ouest-France* and started to read while Granny Soize and I watched television. The rest of the time, he avoided me, spending his days fishing, avenging his self-imposed muteness with me by engaging in expansive conversations with his sailing buddies. And when someone happened to drop in, he would pull the wool over their eyes with a laconic, indulgent comment along the lines of *she's such a sweet little thing*, which just infuriated me all the more. I couldn't stand him, but I never did anything about it. No, instead it was right about then that I started engaging in one idiotic act after another in an attempt to provoke him, the most flamboyant of all having been to leave the earth behind by flying off a cliff in a car.

You might have been forgiven for thinking that the day he gave me that thrashing he was just furious with me for having embarrassed him in front of the whole island. Sadly, it was much more damaging than that. After considering the question from every perspective, I arrived at the following conclusion: he was never able to love himself through me the way he had with my late mother, an exquisite trophy which he would exhibit, saying *that's my wife, have you seen how beautiful she is*. Because that's what my mother was, it seems, a very pretty holiday-maker. A young woman about thirty years his junior whom he had seduced with his tattoos and his sailor's blather. I was born barely six and a half months after they met and I imagine he set sail again the day after I was conceived, because when the matricide happened he had been at sea for five months.

So it was on that infamous day when the gendarmes brought me back that he had kissed me goodbye. I had disappointed him, but the problem is that it all went back to the date of my first breath. My very existence was a disappointment.

Standing there waiting at the end of the jetty, leaning against the railing, taking my place in that long line of women from the island, also allowed me to go back and put myself in Corentine Malgorn's shoes, Corentine, my great-grandmother, who had stood in precisely that spot a century and a half earlier.

The armistice is signed on 26 January 1871. More than six months pregnant and no longer able to conceal her pregnancy, she's watching for boats arriving back to the island, and when sailors come ashore she peppers them feverishly with questions about roads and railways reopening, as well as asking whether any soldiers are returning. January, February, still nothing. At the start of March, suffering from the spitefulness and suffocating stupidity that reigns in such small, insular places, shunned by her own family, who accuse her of having brought shame upon them, she does what everybody with any problem used to do at the time: she goes to see the priest.

'Leave the island, immediately! Take the money from the notary's office and find whoever it was who bought Breval. If he died in the war, he owes you the balance. There are 4000 francs waiting for you at Brest, so go and make something of your life. Just be sure never to return!' That's what she must have been advised by the colossus from the Île Bourbon, because she never set foot on our island again until 1920, at the age of seventy.

Let me just clarify that I did not make him up, that priest. I have described him as he appears in the etchings published in *L'Illustration* at the time of the shipwrecked *Drummond Castle* in 1896 which resulted in 358 deaths.

I also picked up a trace of Corentine's passage to Brest in the minutes of the notarial office of Kersauzon de Pennendreff in the Finistère departmental archives. On 3 March 1871 she received the 4000-franc payment retained by the notary, as witnessed by Breval prior to his departure for the army, and on 6 March the Brest–Paris line reopened all the way through to the Gare Montparnasse.

So there's Corentine Malgorn in a train packed to the rafters, crossing a France that's under full Prussian occupation. She's twenty-one years old. She's wearing a black, calf-length dress that hides her belly, a black, embroidered shawl that shows off her Communion cross and a white bonnet over her short hair. She speaks sufficient French to get by, because until the age of thirteen she attended the convent school, where the nuns taught the language to educate the boys before they joined the Navy. Most importantly, she knows how to read. It's not just that which renders her eminently modern: she is a product of the only matriarchal society in Europe; her life will not, then, tell the story of the men who have trampled over her. She knows only the family name of the people who bought her fiancé. The de Rignys, from Saint-Germain-en-Laye. She is so pregnant she's about to burst, and she has no time to lose.

There's one other trace of her, and quite a significant one at that: her savings book. It was among the family documents piled up in my father's cellar. From it, I learn that she was both wealthy and frugal. That she deposited 3850 francs on 14 March 1871 at the Paris-Montparnasse branch, and another 6000 francs on 26 March, namely a week before my grandfather's birth; that's what made me think that brother-in-law Jules, who had been appointed to buy Botquelen, must have filched some of the money from the de Rignys, seeing as the amount of those two deposits was considerably greater than the 8000-franc price that appeared on the deed of sale.

Five days after the publication of my father's death notice, while I was busy packing up boxes and fighting a furious wish to burn it all, I got a call from my girlfriend Tiphaine, who works at the town hall. Some smooth type in a suit and tie was looking up my family records in the island's births, deaths and marriages register at that very moment.

The death notice I'd posted in *Ouest-France* must have alerted somebody, I said to myself. For somebody to have come all the way to the arsehole of the Iroise, looking for us, the down-and-outters of Brittany, some testamentary panic must have been set off among the authorised representatives of the de Rigny family.

Using the same methodology as you do with families, it's possible to trace a company's genealogy on the internet through the archives of the Trade and Companies Register.

The business known as the Établissements de Rigny at the time my forebear was acquired became De Rigny Construction in 1890 following two capital increases, one of which took place right in the middle of the Prussian occupation. Then it became RGL Construction in 1908, when Ferdinand de Rigny merged with Gireur and Legros from the École Polytechnique, one of whom would go on to marry his daughter.

In the first half of the twentieth century, the company which was now known only as RGL expanded its corporate purpose: in addition to public works, it developed a taste for mining concessions and energy supply. I learnt from another source – the archives of the Purge Commission – that the company, or rather, its manager, Guillaume de Rigny, Ferdinand's youngest son and father of the late Philippe, had various legal issues after the war, struggling to explain how he had managed to effect four capital increases between 1940 and 1944, but it can't have been too serious, as the prosecutor responsible for the file was removed before the matter went anywhere.

RGL continued to expand considerably during the thirty-year post-war economic boom thanks to reconstruction, and then again during the subsequent 'pitiful' thirty years thanks to the oil crisis and its energy business, which was ultimately sold for a fortune in the '90s to some giant in the construction and public works industry, with Philippe de Rigny only keeping the brokerage subsidiary, Oilofina, just to keep some skin in the game.

Seeing as there's only one boat that returns to the mainland in the evening, it was really a very simple task trying to track down a man in a suit on the island; all I had to do was ask anybody at all if they'd seen him. He was busy eating lunch on his own at a table in the single restaurant that was still open in the off season. I went in, greeted the owner and sat down in the chair opposite him.

'It's hard to go unnoticed in such a small place, especially if you're sticking your nose into other people's business. Why are you so interested in my family?'

He told me what I already knew, and I feigned astonishment.

He was acting on behalf of the administrators of the trust which held the assets of a family consisting of two women, a quasi-centenarian and a seventy-two-year-old alcoholic, which was downright disturbing for people who'd been gorging themselves on management fees and risked losing their job.

'What exactly do you want to know?'

'Our office is making unofficial enquiries. The family is not in the know.'

'You haven't answered my question. What do you want to know?'

'Who would benefit under the trust if some misfortune were to befall Marianne de Rigny as well.'

'Okay, you're telling me that the daughter of this woman just died of an overdose, but she herself has no brothers or sisters?'

'She had a brother who was lynched along with his son during a riot in Africa. A truly appalling way to go! And the brother also had a daughter who died in an earthquake in Nepal.'

'An overdose, an earthquake, a lynching, all in the same year! That's some serious curse the family's got going on, I'll say!'

'She also has a twin brother, but the family disowned

him a long time ago. We can't find any trace of him. We don't even know if he's still alive.'

'Disowned? But that doesn't mean anything legally speaking.'

'Agreed, except that the family doesn't want to talk about it. So, except for Marianne, there's nobody left. And then when we put out an alert on the internet, we came across your father's death notice and as it's such an unusual name they sent me here to consult his records, just in case. I traced the family back to a re-transcription of the marriage certificate of your grandfather Renan with his wife, Rose, on which the name Auguste de Rigny is noted as the father of the groom. As all the Parisian records prior to June 1871 went up in smoke, we were unaware of the existence of this direct descendent.'

'I have that certificate. It was in my father's papers.'

'So who's Corentine Malgorn?'

'A damn fine woman. Her photo's on a vault in the cemetery. You can't miss it, it's the most impressive one.'

'So then you must be the great-granddaughter of Auguste de Rigny, the youngest-known beneficiary after Marianne and her twin brother who can't be found.'

'If you say so! Pleased to meet you. I'm Blanche, I'm thirty-eight years old and I have a ten-year-old daughter called Juliette. Voilà. And contrary to any ideas you might get from the way I look, I'm not suffering from any sort of degenerative illness. My ninety-three-year-old great-aunt is in great shape and the only reason my father died recently is because he drowned himself, otherwise he, too, would be in good form. You should organise a cousins' get-together, a *cousinade* as we say around here, so we can introduce ourselves to each other.'

He ignored my comment.

'My board has just asked me to find you, so we're in luck, seeing as you're here. There's something they want to ask you, even if it's a little delicate ...'

'Feel free,' I said with a big smile.

'My bosses want me to ask you the following question, off the record: if there should be some fresh, unexpected misfortune, what would your intentions be vis-à-vis the trust?'

'It involves some tax optimisation thing on an island paradise with palm trees, right?'

'Yes, in the British Virgin Islands.'

'If this family pays people to look after their wealth and those people take it upon themselves to send somebody all this way, just to consult the births, deaths and marriages register, that must mean we're talking about enormous sums of money, right?'

'Yes.'

'I'm really fond of island life. That's what you should tell your bosses. Maybe that'll make them feel better ...'

A few days earlier, on the occasion of the Prussian parade down the Champs-Élysées, Jules Vallès had published an editorial in *Le Cri du Peuple* which had moved Auguste to his core.

'Do not fire at them, Republicans, do not fire because they want you to fire. And do not allow yourself to be killed, heroic coward, when there is still much to be done; when as our country mourns, there is a revolution underway.'

'An heroic coward. That's what I am. An heroic coward.' His steps beat time to the oxymoron as he made his way home through the dark, gas having made only niggardly appearances since the lifting of the siege. He had just left the Tivoli-Vauxhall theatre where meetings of the National Guard central committee were being held. Off he went, every evening, boiling over with conviction and passion, consumed by the need to act, wishing desperately that he might be called on to defend the glory of the Commune. But there again, while he begged for responsibility in this new army of Communards, the old revolutionaries from 1848 continued to reject him in an amiable fashion, calling him *whippersnapper* or *young 'un*, and promising him that one day his turn would come. True, he admired them, some having endured solitary confinement or deportation, but the guarded caution of their arguments he found acted as a dampener on his own eagerness.

At the top of Boulevard Magenta, he noticed small groups of soldiers appearing here and there through the evening mist, gripping their rifles with both hands as if departing for the front. 'But where are they all going?' the young man wondered, leaning against a building in Place du Château d'Eau. He encountered others in Rue Saint-Denis, similarly silent, swift, inscrutable. He decided to do an about-face and follow them discreetly, keeping to the building façades from one carriage entrance to the next. In this fashion he made his way up the boulevard, all the way to the hill of Montmartre, where other groups of soldiers were converging from the direction of Rue Mercadet and Rue Mont-Cenis. Hundreds of soldiers.

From where he was standing, he could see the slopes of the Butte Montmartre, where he witnessed men from the engineering corps busy demolishing the protective barriers surrounding the cannons under the direction of a general on horseback.

'They're removing our artillery!' he murmured softly to himself.

He started running, breathlessly climbing the hill until he reached the Solferino tower, where he knew a group of National Guards were on duty. There, at the foot of the building, lay a man in uniform, with a woman dressed in grey skirts and black corset leaning over him. It was Louise Michel, whom he recognised from the numerous times he had heard her speak at the Tivoli-Vauxhall.

'Citizen, Thiers' troops are disarming the Champ des

Polonais at Montmartre. What should I do?'

'Follow me,' she replied. 'We must alert the city!'

And he set off after her, hurtling down the Butte Montmartre, gathering up every passer-by he encountered who happened to have ventured out for their morning bread or milk. Having made it to the bottom of the hill, he started beating on every door he passed, rounding up as many people as possible.

'We are being disarmed by Versailles … They're withdrawing the cannons from the Champ des Polonais …'

Auguste felt strong, alive, capable of decisive and timely action, ready to rouse all Paris singlehandedly. At last, here he was in the thick of things.

Already the streets were filling with people, aghast, who in turn set off to warn others. He saw Louise Michel, who was well known in the neighbourhood, shouting 'Treason!' at the top of her lungs.

And word ricocheted about until a riotous mob had gathered.

The crowd grew denser with every passing minute, surrounding the square and preventing the teams of horses from getting through. General Lecomte, whose name Auguste had picked up from the jeers flying thick and fast from every quarter, ordered the regulars to remove the cannons by hand and to form a path with their rifles to allow the horses through, but every time a cannon was harnessed up, the housewives would cut the traces with their kitchen knives. Slowly the crowd, comprising mostly women and children, regained possession of them, overwhelming the soldiers. Wild with rage, Lecomte ordered them to fire on the civilians. 'Rifle butts in the air!' shouted one of his officers, refusing to fire, as his general, frothing at the mouth, threatened him with the firing squad. By half past eight in the morning, it was all over.

Intoxicated by the action, by the revolutionary rhetoric, Auguste lingered in the area for a few hours, then decided to head home. He was keen to recount the story of the stealthy arrival of the soldiers to his aunt, to describe the difficulties faced by the teams of horses, the way men had fraternised with the people, but especially his role in helping Louise Michel trigger the day's events, a day that would surely go down in the annals of history. He made his way back down Rue des Martyrs against the flow of curious onlookers heading up to Montmartre, only arriving back at Rue du 4 Septembre towards midday.

'Aunt, I must tell you ... it was extraordinary!' he said, fervently.

The apartment looked like a battlefield, as if burglars had just departed. Clothilde and her maid, Rosalie, were busy frantically packing their valises with as much as they would carry.

'But what is happening? Where are you going?'

'When I heard that the cannons were being removed, you can imagine I had to go out. As I made my way to Montmartre, I saw barricades being erected all over the place and soldiers fleeing towards Concorde. Thiers has decided to depart for Versailles with the government immediately; that is all I need to know. I'm going back to Saint-Germain!

Do help us carry this to the Gare Saint-Lazare.'

'But Aunt! I was there. At Montmartre ... The atmosphere was very amicable. Only a single shot was fired and that was by a regular soldier.'

'Well, I was at Place Pigalle and the scoundrels I saw ... You can't imagine! They could already smell chaos. They took two generals prisoner and there is talk of their execution. The entire town will succumb to the insurrection and I know from a reliable source that troops are falling back to Versailles. Tomorrow we shall be delivered up to the frenzy of the people. We must hurry, Rosalie! Run off ahead! Go, secure the tickets. No matter the class, we must take the next train before they storm them all. Wait for me at the end of platform 3.'

Stunned, Auguste dashed after his aunt. Struggling under the weight of the packages, they saw more panic-stricken bourgeois families in Rue Auber carrying all the clothes they had been able to pack piled onto their backs, pushcarts filled to the brim with valises and knick-knacks, as well as a few hansom cabs pulled by the rare horses who were fortunate enough not to have been eaten. All were converging on the Gare Saint-Lazare.

'Hurry, Auguste, it's mayhem already!'

'Hurry? This weighs a tonne! What is it you have in there?'

'My silverware.'

'You are quite mad!'

Rosalie, who had managed to secure them seats in second

class, was waiting for Clothilde at the agreed place.

Auguste settled his aunt into her compartment. She took him by the arm and addressed him seriously before the train moved off.

'You are a young, impassioned fool, my dear nephew, and I am fond of you just as you are because you make me laugh. But enough now. Things are serious. I am intimately acquainted with Thiers; you can believe me when I tell you: he will kill you all ... all of you Communards, if only for having dared to unnerve the bourgeoisie.'

It was at Chatou, as the train was emptying out, that Clothilde noticed her.

It must be said, it was hard not to. Resembling nothing Clothilde had ever seen before, the woman was sitting bolt upright, squeezed between the shambolic piles of valises that were fit to bursting with frills and ornaments, and apparently utterly unaware of the political events that had them all fleeing Paris.

'Who might she be?' wondered Clothilde. 'One of those good Breton housemaids whom the bourgeoisie of Seine-et-Oise are so very keen on engaging to care for their children? And why does she not have any luggage?' She whispered something into Rosalie's ear, who shook her head to answer 'No', discreetly indicating with her chin the woman's rounded belly: she was large with child and seemed not at all ashamed. Indeed, she appeared to be radiating dignity.

She did not disembark in Pecq either, which intrigued Clothilde further still.

Suddenly, when they were no more than a few kilo-metres from their destination, the young woman leaned towards her and said:

'Good day, Madame, if I might be so bold. You are head-ing to Saint-Germain-en-Laye and seem quite the grand lady. My name is Corentine Malgorn and I have travelled a great distance. I am looking for a family of some repute, the de Rignys, for whom my fiancé was a substitute. Might you know where they live?'

'Oh, my heavens!' Clothilde was unable to contain her-self.

11

AS FAR AS I COULD REMEMBER, I had only ever set foot on Rue du Faubourg-Saint-Honoré on one previous occasion, a local public heritage day when I had visited the Hôtel de Rigny, a splendid mansion house gifted to the widow of Casimir and Clothilde's brother in 1867. The taxi had dropped me off in Place Beauvau due to an official motorcade leaving the Élysée palace, so I had taken the chance to walk back up the street on foot, and even if there was nothing for me in all the high-end boutiques I walked past, it was a complete treat for the eyes to be able to admire the artisanal skills on display for those able to afford their work. So I took my time and wandered slowly towards the private clubhouse of the Cercle de l'Union Interalliée.

I had had the idea a few days earlier of messaging the late Alice de Rigny's boyfriend, the bespectacled hipster, through Instagram, because I thought it might be one way of discovering the end to my hero's story: after all, it was no coincidence that he and his two friends had chosen my island to honour the memory of their friend and girlfriend by tossing teddy bears from the cliffs into the sea.

Auguste, unlike my grandfather Botquelen, was no *res nullius,* abandoned in a ditch. He was the son of a well-to-do family. And they do not disappear just like that.

Intrigued, he replied immediately to my little DM and we met in a café downstairs from my place. When he saw me sitting there with my crutches leaning up against the edge of the table, he had a moment of panic, thinking it was some sordid pick-up plan, then he had a change of heart, as my appearance and face prompted a vague memory.

'Do I know you?'

'No, but we've seen each other before. It was last winter, your girlfriend had just died and you had come on a pilgrimage to the island where I live. I decided to contact you because I wanted to ask you why you chose to go there in particular, and not somewhere else?'

'But who are you?'

So I gave him my family history, leaving out the 'eavesdropping' part when we had all been on the boat together which had kicked off my investigations.

'So, let me reiterate my question: in your opinion, does this family know we even exist?'

'To be honest, I'd be surprised if they did, otherwise I would have heard them talking about you and also, knowing them, if they had found out at the time that one of their own had officially recognised a newborn who was not from their social class, they would have had him knocked off quick smart. Especially as, if I've understood correctly, your grandfather was legitimately able to claim his share of the inheritance. And when it comes to money, frankly, nothing gets in these people's way as far as I can tell.'

'So what was it all about, that pilgrimage? Just coincidence?'

'Not really, no! We had said that one day we'd all go there as a bit of a private joke. Alice had a book at her place that came from her parents. The sort of self-published literary shit spouted out by some family ancestor that you feel obliged to keep at the back of your bookshelf for generation after generation. She used to say it had been her sexual education and sometimes, to give us a laugh, she would read us passages from it. It describes the absolutely filthy details of an orgy that takes place over several days during which sex-starved Amazons force themselves on some poor explorer. They squeeze every last drop from him and he ends up dying from exhaustion and ecstasy having inseminated every girl of childbearing age. A sort of pornographic Jules Verne: *The Adventures of Count Mogador in the Land of the Amazons* by a certain Jules de Brassac. And the action takes place on your island.'

'Well, would you look at that, he passed completely under my radar,' I thought to myself.

'And your girlfriend's aunt and grandmother, do you ever see them?'

'Not at all. I only ever caught a glimpse of them on the yacht where Adrienne would host her parties. Nobody in that family was ever very interested in me. But if you want to see them, it's not hard. The old lady has lunch every day at the Cercle de l'Union Interalliée clubhouse. I know because I took Alice there on my scooter several times when she had to be on duty. Don't turn up in jeans. Apparently that's a complete no-no.'

I went into the courtyard of the mansion house, and when

they asked who I was I simply gave them my name and said I was there to have lunch with my great-aunt. Nobody asked me another thing and I was smoothly directed to a terrace overlooking magnificent gardens.

'Madame de Rigny said she wished to dine in the garden as it's such a beautiful day. She'll be here in a few minutes, while her daughter parks the car in the courtyard.'

Finding myself surrounded by all this beauty, I let out a sigh of contentment, noting in surprise the ease with which I was adapting to the comforts money can procure.

Yvonne, the almost-centenarian, arrived on the arm of a butler, who deposited her delicately on a chair opposite mine with the same caution one might deploy handling a priceless antique vase.

'Your great-niece is already here. She's waiting for you.'

'Perfect, perfect!'

She seemed delighted to see me or, more accurately, the hundreds of facelifts she'd had meant that her perpetually wide-open eyes and mouth, the latter pulled into an eternal smile, lent her the radiant look of a woman who was completely off with the fairies.

'Is everything alright, pet?'

It was surreal.

'Yes, aunt. I've come to see you because I'm planning on writing a sort of family history, but I'm missing the ending.'

'The ending?'

At this, her mind must have wandered off, because she repeated the word several times with a beatific smile.

Not a great start.

Suddenly, just as Tata and I were sitting there getting along just fine, the silhouette of an enormous piss-pot, the spitting image of Adrienne but with an added thirty years and thirty kilos, and with the same Tagada-strawberry-flavoured e-cigarette hanging from her mouth, blocked out the sun.

'And who are you?'

'My name's Blanche de Rigny and as I was just telling your mother, I'm looking into our family history and, in particular, our common forebear, Auguste, the brother of your great-grandfather, Ferdinand.'

While I was speaking I pulled out my ID, which she fiddled with, looking completely dazed and confused.

'Common with who? What? Is it money you want?'

'No, not at all, I only wanted to ask you – well, you or your brother – if you know when and in what circumstances the notorious Auguste died, because there's nothing in his records at births, deaths and marriages, and so obviously it's complicated trying to work out what happened to him ...'

'My brother died in Africa.'

'I'm talking about your other brother; your twin brother, Pierre.'

At that, her wino's eyes glazed over with rage and she brought her face so close to mine that the ethylene coming from her breath pretty well singed my skin. Her entire body reeked of alcohol like an old sponge that had been used to soak up a puddle of cheap booze.

'How dare you!'

'Pierre? Pierre, have you come back?' said the old girl, happily. 'Pierre, come and say hello to *maman* ...'

It was full on.

I didn't pursue the matter. I retrieved my ID and stood up before anybody was tempted to throw me out.

'I'll sue the pants off you! You'll get nothing, not a cent!' I heard her yell after me.

When I got to the front steps, I asked the parking valet to point out Madame's car, saying I was worried I had forgotten something on the back seat. He gestured to an enormous Bentley. I went over to it, pretending to peer inside, noted down the number plate and took a discreet photo of the car with my phone.

Because, more than anything, I cannot stand being treated badly, and I wanted to teach that horrible woman a lesson.

Back at work, the minute one of the court clerks had her back turned, I consulted the records of Marianne de Rigny on CASSIOPEE, the digital platform used by police, prosecutors and judges to store information about an accused. As I had suspected, she was a regular at what we like to call *the muscadet hearings*. She had been sentenced seven times for driving under the influence, receiving a three-month suspended sentence for the second to last one and, for the most recent one, a three-month custodial sentence but with no warrant for detention, which still didn't stop her driving while she was pissed.

The next one would be the one.

I asked Dioulou, the guy who ran my team of couriers and the only one with a residence permit, to follow her on his bike when she emerged from the Club and to fake an accident, and then to hail the police at the top of his lungs.

Twenty-four hours later, she was brought before the courts for summary trial, where, in full delirium tremens, she rained insults on the chief magistrate.

I was sitting at the back of the court and when she caught sight of me, she let out a sort of telluric bawling sound, something that seemed to emerge from the depths of time to fill the space, and which indicated to me that she had understood. Understood what exactly, I couldn't say, but she must have taken it damned poorly, because when added to the death of her daughter, the six-month custodial sentence she had just been served as well as the revocation of the three-month suspended sentence and detention order for her prior three-month custodial, she hanged herself in her cell using her Hermès belt, which a cop who was either negligent or simply terrified had forgotten to remove from her.

When I suddenly saw the journalists abandon their positions outside a media-friendly trial to run in a tight huddle towards the entrance to the cells, I said to myself that the only pure truths were life and death. The rest was just subjective crap, waffle, blather.

That's what I said to myself.

Paris
2 April 1871

'Thank God nobody saw me come in,' thought Auguste while the priest of Notre-Dame des Victoires murmured Latin phrases and sprinkled his poor son with holy water. The widow Malgorn had firmly insisted on the christening and he had had no choice but to agree and suffer in silence.

To see Corentine and the Breton godmother she had chosen repeating the incantations of the man of the cloth with their beatific smiles reminded him of the conversation he had had two months earlier with his aunt Clothilde about the dispiriting results of the legislative elections.

'But what were you thinking? That France consists of nothing more than the Grands Boulevards?'

'But, Aunt, we're talking about the first elections of the new Republic ... Some brilliant men were running: Hugo, Gambetta, Quinet, Rochefort ... But no, they elect an Assembly that's 60 per cent monarchist ... How can such a thing still be possible in 1871?'

'Because France is a nation of small-minded country bumpkins who want order, God, peace and the reassuring framework of its traditions: its king, its comitia and its ridiculous little balls held for the Festival of Saint John that I have such a horror of. Thiers is the only person able to understand it and who knows how to make himself acceptable.'

She was right: that snake with glasses, *the friend of the*

family, had been elected by the *country bumpkins* and by considerable majority.

He did not resent this unfortunate war widow for being sanctimonious, he was irritated with the priests for having held the people in this infantile state for so long. 'Let him make the most of this cult of his while he can,' he said to himself as he observed the officiating priest. A few more weeks and they would be done with this foolish, stultifying ritual, and the churches of Paris would be transformed into places for the people. Yes, he had conceded this Mass, but he had resolutely refused to allow his name to appear on the baptismal register.

Once the benediction had concluded, all that remained was for him to suffer the interminable Credo and he would be done with this deplorable ceremony. Then, as a family, they would cross the street to the town hall of the 2nd arrondissement, where Perrachon and Trousselier were waiting for them, this time for a real baptism – a Republican one.

Credo in Deum, Patrem omnipotentem, Creatorem caeli et terrae... Et in Jesum Christum, Filium eius unicum, Dominum nostrum...

Auguste thought about all the events that had taken place at such a disturbing pace these last two weeks.

On the 20th day of March, namely two days after the business with the cannons where he had distinguished himself, he had received a summons from his father accompanied by numerous threats calling for him to return to Saint-Germain-en-Laye. In response, he had enlisted in the National Guard, ready to lay down his life for the Commune, and this time they had accepted him. Needless to say, his family had not taken kindly to his decision and had resolved to cut him off completely. He had not removed his Communard uniform since, except for this foolish christening where he had appeared in civilian dress so he would go unremarked.

... qui conceptus est de Spiritu Sancto, natus ex Maria Virgine, passus sub Pontio Pilato, crucifixus, mortuus, et sepultus, descendit ad inferos ...

On the 25th, he had received a note from his aunt informing him of the appearance of Corentine Malgorn at Saint-Germain-en-Laye, as well as the resulting enormous family dispute as to the balance payment for his replacement: Ferdinand and Jules on the one hand, Casimir and his wife on the other, and Berthe in the middle of it all, unable to stop weeping and feeling faint: Clothilde had found it all highly entertaining and had defended the war widow's interests tooth and nail, good patriot that she was. Her little note had concluded with these few mysterious sentences: *She speaks French and can thus provide you with more information as to the identity of the man who died in your stead. I know it means a good deal to you. For pity's sake, refrain from the foolish act I suspect you will be tempted to commit.* It was followed by the address of a boarding house in Montparnasse.

... tertia die resurrexit a mortuis, ascendit ad caelos, sedet ad dexteram ...

With an elbow to his ribs, the mother of his son called him to order as he massacred the Credo with his out of time and incomprehensible monotonous chanting.

... Dei Patris omnipotentis, inde venturus est iudicare vivos et mortuos.

He had set off immediately to look for the address she had provided and it was only when he saw her standing before him, on the verge of giving birth, that he understood his aunt's message. Happiness had radiated from him like the sun.

While the fiacre waited outside her boarding house, Auguste deployed a wealth of imagination to persuade her to follow him to his aunt's residence, but she contented herself with listening to him with her arms crossed without so much as raising an eyebrow. Nonetheless, after half an hour of to-ing and fro-ing, it was the words *water closet with running water* that won the day and meant he could bring the young widow back to Rue du 4 Septembre, where she gave birth to a son.

As for the Breval Botquelen episode, she had absolutely nothing further to recount except to say: 'Well, he was a man, what else is there to say ...' 'He was indeed brave ...' Or 'it is truly sad what happened to him ...' No romantic impulses, no lover's sorrow, nothing. As if the woman had not expected anything of the poor lad but that he be the progenitor of her child. As to general conversation, it was hardly any better. When he had sought her political opinions, she had replied, 'All I really want is to be able to eat my soup in peace, set up a fine business and above all else cause no trouble to the Good Lord,' in that ghastly accent reeking of muddy earth.

Pious, unintelligent, and a likely adherent to the royalist Chouan peasant movements, Corentine was, in her own way, somewhat puzzling; at once very free-spirited, and yet quite the antithesis of the type of emancipated woman with whom he was rubbing shoulders at the barricades on a daily basis.

... Credo in Spiritum Sanctum, sanctam Ecclesiam catholicam, sanctorum communionem, remissionem peccatorum, carnis resurrectionem vitam aeternam.

Amen.

'There we go, it's done, let us be off!' said Auguste, steering the two Breton women towards the door.

They complied ungraciously, and not without casting him a dark look for having ushered them out of the church.

At the door to the town hall, they were greeted by Perrachon and Trousselier, dressed in their National Guard uniforms, and by an old unkempt revolutionary poet from 1848, Eugène Pottier, the new mayor of the 2nd arrondissement. The latter offered Corentine a bouquet of red carnations as he bestowed upon her a *Greetings, citizen*, which caused her no end of displeasure.

They then went into the reception room of the town hall. Auguste had, for the occasion, prepared a speech rich in obscure rhetoric involving the Mother Country, anti-capitalism and the tyranny of commodities, but he could not find his notes. The ceremony thus boiled down to a recitation of Pottier's poem 'L'Enfant', performed by the author himself, which finished with:

> *Mother, mother, the time is nigh*
> *Come drape with your red flag*
> *The cradle of your new child*

Then it was time to note the parentage on the register of births, deaths and marriages.

'So, what is this little citizen to be called?' the mayor enquired of its parents.

'Renan,' said Corentine. 'I want to call him Renan.'

'Your father's name, no doubt...'

'No, it is nobody's name. It's the name I have chosen for him!'

Auguste intervened: 'When the ceremony is over, my comrades and I will be joining forces with Duval and Flourens to defend Paris. In recognition of this action, I wish him to have Astyanax as his second name.'

'Excellent,' said the poet.

'What sort of a name is that?' asked the widow, frowning.

'It is the name of the son Hector takes in his arms before leaving to defend Troy against the Greek troops of Achilles.'

'Who is this Hector?'

'Are you familiar with Ronsard? A poet, just like Monsieur here.'

'No.'

'In his epic poem he tells how Astyanax, the son of Hector, having escaped death by moving the Greeks with his beauty, undertakes to journey to Gaul at the request of the gods, where he then establishes France.'

Corentine turned to the mayor.

'Did you know that? That God sent Asty-whatever-his-name-is to establish France?'

'Absolutely!'

'Well then, that's alright with me.'

Everybody signed the register and Corentine asked for and was provided with a copy of her son's birth certificate so she might have him registered on her internal passport in the event she decided to return home with him.

Once the Republican ceremony had finished, Auguste changed out of his clothes in the back room and emerged clad in his National Guard uniform onto the forecourt of the town hall, where the others were waiting. There he took little Astyanax from his mother's arms and brandished him heavenwards:

'O Jupiter and all ye immortal gods, may my son be illustrious. Render him strong and courageous that he might reign over and command Troy, so that one day every man shall cry out upon seeing him return from combat: "He is braver still than his father!"'

Then he returned the child to his mother and disappeared around the corner.

12

IT WAS CAUSING THE TRUST a huge headache, everything that was going on; I was not yet heir to the de Rignys, but I was the only one left to look after the old woman, so in return for a monthly salary equivalent to what I would earn in a year they begged me to move into a sort of three-storey apartment on Avenue Foch that had an internal staircase of the kind you see on cruise liners as well as a vast roof garden.

Hildegarde, who no longer had a job after being sentenced, moved in with me and Juliette, bringing along two very ugly dogs, Pistachio and Geranium, whom she had hastened to retrieve from animal rescue. We also had the most engineered rabbit in France, the only phosphorescent descendant of Alba who was cloned with a jellyfish in 2000, as well as an ailing sheep who had been rescued that same day during a raid on a genetic engineering laboratory.

Old Yvonne was nice enough and felt comfortable surrounded by animals, but my goal was to track down her son, Pierre, and apart from telling me he had been wicked for having chosen another mother whenever I would show her family photographs that had had his head meticulously cut out, she was of no help to us whatsoever.

We searched the whole apartment, shook out every book, tipped out every drawer, went down to the cellar and through the cupboards. Nothing.

Juliette, with her usual pugnacity, and taking advantage of the few moments of Tata's relative lucidity after she had stuffed herself with cake, tried relentlessly, night after night, to extract something more from her.

'Is his new *maman* pretty?' she would ask her, showing her once again the image of a headless Pierre, aged twenty.

In that photo, which was dated February 1968 on the reverse, he was posing next to his late twin sister, Marianne, on a beach at Cannes. It was the last known photo of him in the family album, the next one having simply been ripped out.

'No, she's very old.'

'As old as you?'

'Older.'

'So why is there a gap here? What was the photo that used to be there?'

'That was the one Pierre took to send to her.'

'Pierre ripped out one of the photos from this album to send to his new mother?'

'Yes, he's wicked, he ruined my album.'

This was going to take some work.

One evening when I couldn't get to sleep, thinking about the time I had discovered the whole de Rigny story by just googling words I'd happened to snatch from a conversation between strangers on a boat, I tried my luck once again by typing in the words 'mother', '1968', 'old', 'sent his photo'.

Page 1:
 stuff about pregnancy in older women;
 Whatever happened to the girls from May '68?;
 Cameroon: an old dead woman wakes up at her funeral.
 68 people trampled;
 the progressive integration of the working mother ...
Nothing.
Page 2:
 cinema, modelling;
 revolution of the older woman;
 an extract from a thirteenth-century fable;
 a story from BFM News about a seventy-nine-year-old
Belgian grandmother caught by speed camera doing 238
kilometres an hour in her Porsche;
 Mother's Agenda, written in French, free e-book.

I clicked on that last hit and was directed to a page suggest-
ing I download the thirteen volumes of the journey of the
Mother towards eternal life by way of her yoga of the cells,
a record of interviews collated by her disciple, Satprem.
The first page of the website showed a photograph of
Mother, an extremely old woman with a benevolent smile,
who had founded Auroville in 1968, north of Pondicherry,
recruiting young people from all over Europe based on
their photos, and in particular young people from France,
since she, too, was French.
 I got up and went to see Tata in her bedroom at the
other end of the apartment. On the way I crossed paths
with Jelly, the fluorescent rabbit, who went mad every
night dashing from one room to the next at full throttle

like one of those glow-in-the-dark balls sold by Pakis out-side the big department stores.

She looked a bit freaky when she was asleep, the old bag. A bit like an Egyptian mummy. Given all the facelifts she'd had, she was no longer able to close her eyes, and because she tended to look like a little bundle of dried twigs when she was in bed, you never knew if she was dead or alive.

'Tata, is this her? Pierre's wicked *maman*?' I asked her, showing her the screenshot on my mobile of Mirra Alfassa, otherwise known as Mother. 'Is she the one he sent his photo to?'

Suddenly very distressed, she grabbed my arm in a dis-play of unbelievable strength and sent my phone flying to the floor ...

'She took my little boy ... It was his birthday ... She kept him in India even though it was his birthday ...'

'Pierre's in India?'

She rattled off a few more phrases in a similar vein before slumping back onto her bed with a moan of genuine suffering. She finally released her claw-like grip and sank back into contemplation of the patterns on the *toile de Jouy* stretched over her bedroom walls.

I'd found him.

We left Yvonne and the animals in the care of numerous omnipresent staff who, after a life of subjection by that abominable family, were quite happy to put up with a bit more eccentricity and so didn't see any problem with having to pick up the sheep and rabbit droppings in the apartment, and left for Pondicherry on the hunt for the last of the living de Rignys – apart from me and Juliette, of course.

But before we left, we all sat down to watch an old documentary from 1968 about the setting up of Auroville. In response to the French TV journalist who had travelled halfway around the world to ask all those young fanatics what could possibly have been going through their minds to ditch everything to go and join a guru in the far reaches of Tamil Nadu in India, they all declared, one after the other, 'We answered Mother's call to come and live the great adventure.' Each one of them had a radiant face.

Juliette was fascinated by a small blonde girl about her age who was being followed by the camera. She spoke fluent English, French, German, Hindi and Tamil, switching from one language to the other as she answered the journalist's questions.

'What will you do after this?'

'Mother will decide. As I might choose something which wouldn't be good for me, it's better that Mother decides.'

'Will you have children when you're older?'

'Mother said it's better not to have children. Mother says we have to do something new.'

'But Mother won't always be there to tell you what to do …'

'Mother will always be here.'

The young girl recounted how she was going to Last School, the first step on the way to No School, as required by Mother. A person you might call a teacher explained that the Free Progress school was not designed to produce ready-made consumers, but rather to reveal to a child the truth of their being and to inspire their curiosity, so she would be capable of choosing what was right for her as an adult ... And Juliette, who was always bored to tears in class, thought that was way too cool.

The documentary concluded with images of Christ-like, thin, bearded, long-haired men passing buckets of earth to each other on a huge construction site against a backdrop of the setting sun. Then came Mother's warm, maternal voice over a panning shot that took in their serene faces: *There are people who love adventure and I am addressing them when I issue this appeal: 'Let me invite you on this great adventure.' I know nothing of what will happen to you tomorrow. You must abandon everything you anticipated, everything you have planned, everything you have built, and set off on a journey into the unknown. And let come what may!*

At that point, Tata started pointing her finger at the computer screen and screaming in a tone that was no longer the incoherent babbling nor the kindly granny tone we were familiar with. No, it was pure de Rigny, out and out.

'Silly fool! Come home this instant!'

So that is where Pierre had gone at the age of twenty. He had set off on *the great adventure* to join up with men and women who had adopted the common values of material detachment, abandonment of ego and a gift economy, with the aim of reaching a new form of consciousness.

How could you resist such a thing six months after the publication of Guy Debord's *The Society of the Spectacle*?

Especially knowing that it wasn't some bizarre, sectarian nonsense but an experiment that had been launched with great pomp and ceremony by UNESCO, which had sent delegates from one hundred and twenty-one countries to the community's inauguration.

The documentary helped me understand why the de Rignys had completely disowned their son, Pierre. Because Money, the only language spoken by that family, had proved powerless to find the words to convince him to stay. So, having arrived at a point of being unable to communicate at all, you might as well just be done with it.

The trust didn't hold back for Juliette's and my first time in an aeroplane: three seats in business on an A380. We travelled in a bedroom on the top deck of a flying monster. I didn't sleep and nor did my daughter. We stretched out on our sides, glued to each other, heads on a pillow watching the sun rise over a sea of clouds. It was magical. Hildegarde, for her part, was hardcore anti-flying because of the carbon footprint of planes. She slept like a log with her feet hanging over the end of the bed by 40 centimetres, snoring to top it all off.

On arrival in Chennai, and just a stone's throw from the airport, we copped a dose of India smack in the face: the oxcarts, the colours, the destitution, the thousands of scooters and motorcycles, the millions of cars, the unbreathable air, the heat, the rubbish, the enormous birds, the cripples, the Middle Ages with mobile phones, cows on the loose, more heat, horns blaring, people shitting in the street ... it took a lot more than that to unnerve me and Hildegarde; death, suffering, the lack of any normality, and the deformity … we knew it all by heart. As for Juliette, provided she wasn't being served up dodgy, distorted notions of reality, she was happy. But it came as no surprise to me that so many innocent tourists totally lose it after a few days in this country and end up completely prostrate in a corner of their hotel room, in acute decompensation.

After four hours on the road, India all of a sudden stopped being India and gave way to the peacefulness of the forest, with rows of white pyramids emerging from the vegetation, giant mushrooms punctured by windows, structures in the shape of flying saucers, and old VW Kombi vans, their faded bodywork hinting at the journey from Europe in the '70s. White people everywhere. Tourists wandering around in ethno-chic clothes and busy-looking Aurovillians getting about on motorbikes with blond kids sitting behind them, hair blowing in the wind.

We'd made it.

On the way there, I had read that Auroville was the most significant reforestation and soil regeneration pro-gram in the world and that the pioneers had planted 2 million trees in that red, arid soil where previously there had been absolutely nothing. As a result, numerous species of birds and animals had returned, accelerating the dissemina-tion of seeds and creating a truly gigantic forest with its own microclimate. It was true, it felt less hot than elsewhere and the surrounding natural landscape was spectacular.

We spent the following days on mopeds going from village to village, each with a name like Truth, Contemplation,

Certainty, Courage or Solitude, and asking every French person we met if they knew a Pierre who hadn't been home since the place was set up. It didn't take us long to track him down, seeing as the French adult community numbered only 350 Aurovillians, a handful of whom had been pioneers and were still alive. We were told that he no longer went by that name because Mother had given him another, and that he was living in a place called Dream in the Green Belt. That he was a taciturn man, that he lived in a house tucked away in the trees and that he never saw anybody.

When we arrived at his place on our putt-putting scooters, he was busy repairing a chainsaw that was on its last legs. He was skeleton-thin, with a face like sundried leather, but he was in great shape, barefoot, dressed only in an old pair of grease-stained shorts, his long, grey hair pulled back in a ponytail.

He watched us in silence as we got off our mopeds.

With the aging-Christ look he had going on, he exuded an air of majestic detachment, like a metaphysical emanation, which I found a little unsettling, but all good, I didn't allow myself to be thrown off but instead got straight to it. I introduced myself, summarised my findings and described in minute detail the misfortunes that had befallen his family. I spoke for a long time while he remained silent, scrutinising my face with that wary look which told me within two minutes that even if he hadn't confirmed his identity, I had found the right person, such was the resemblance to his late sister, despite his considerably fewer kilos and his fifty years of living in India.

In the meantime, Juliette, who incidentally had sworn she would chain herself to a tree if we tried to take her back to France, had started patting a creature three times her own size outside the house, a creature with a ridge of sorts that I ended up identifying with a great deal of difficulty as a domesticated Indian boar. Hildegarde, for her part, had gone off to take a good look around the property with her usual brazenness.

At one point, when I had finished telling my story and he still hadn't opened his mouth, I finally lost my patience.

'Don't you have anything to say? Nothing you want to ask me? Like *how's Mum?*' I asked him, ironically.

'How's Mum?' he repeated, his face fixed in a grimace.

'She's on the way out, but she's hanging in there.'

'Super.'

'Is that it?'

'You've come to me here, in the middle of the forest, to tell me about a family I haven't thought about for half a century and to let me know that all its members have died … It's a bit much, isn't it?'

'I acknowledge, it is a bit much. I should have been a little more tactful, but it's not really my strong suit, being tactful.'

'That's not the point. When he was really little, my brother was already beating up the weakest kids so he could take things from them that he would only throw out later on. Our father was the same. He couldn't stand people having something he didn't have: mistresses, properties, businesses, horses, it was the same with everything. My mother was the jealous guardian of this nightmarish temple. As for my sister, she was just always trying to get all these weirdos to fall in love with her, but that didn't work out too well for her because by seventeen she was doing her first alcohol detox and rehab. And the others, well, I didn't even know they existed … no … I just find it surprising, that's all.'

'Find what surprising?'

'That five people from one family die within a few months of each other … A convenient outcome, don't you think?'

I could have been indignant, put on an act, but I remained impassive because for once I felt I shouldn't lie. So I said nothing.

'Is it the money you want? Is that it?'

'Yes.'

'And what would you do with it?'

'Bring legal proceedings against polluting companies, engage in political lobbying and manipulate public opinion via social media. These days you can make people believe just about anything, it's just a question of having the funds. My friend Hildegarde had the idea – using expert scientific evidence to support it – of putting the notion out there that the consumption of intensively farmed animals is the principal cause of the Alzheimer's boom, due to toxins in the animals' flesh resulting from the suffering they're forced to endure their whole lives. And if we throw everything at it, I can guarantee you that after a few months there'll be as many meat-eaters left as there are smokers. We'll do the same with the handful of businesses that are responsible for almost 70 per cent of global warming. Tonnes of legal proceedings are in the process of being initiated and we're starting to see results, especially those brought against agri-businesses. The convictions are even resulting in good pay-outs. We're going to flush out victims from all around the world so they can file proceedings. We'll pay for the best lawyers for them and pay for the expert witnesses just like the companies have always done. We'll create the divine anarchy Mother has always dreamt of; you can't refuse, because it's what Mother would have wanted.'

At that he started to laugh like a madman, then he started up his chainsaw.

'You're pretty devious, aren't you!'

And he made a move towards my daughter.

I completely freaked out; I was powerless, with my crutches sinking into the loose earth. I couldn't call Hilde-garde, who was now too far away and who wouldn't have heard me shouting over the noise of the machine.

Juliette, however, was not at all frightened as she watched him approach.

'Don't touch that tree!'

'It's heading for my house with the lianas it's putting down into the soil to form new trunks. Move out of the way, I have to cut it down.'

'No!'

'And why not? I'm the one who planted it! I can't see why it should be forcing me out of my own house.'

'It provides shade and it's a home for the birds. You, on the other hand, you don't do anything useful.'

'That's not true! I've planted and nurtured thousands of plants just like it.'

'Yes, but now they're managing just fine on their own and this one here wants you to let it grow where it pleases. You're not going to cut it down, that's all there is to it, or else you'll have to saw through me too!'

And she clung to the trunk like a koala.

Ten years old and five years of Tata Hildi's activism.

He switched off the motor and turned back to me.

'And how did you get this idea of saving the world into your head?'

'Looking at the protest marches in the street below my apartment. Every time I wondered how you could really change things instead of implementing initiatives that systematically make people take to the streets. And then, when I was researching our ancestor, Auguste, I came across a quote from Flaubert that's as contemptuous as it is relevant: "The people accept any tyrant provided they're allowed to keep their snouts in the trough." Every time it's taken away from them – the trough, that is – the populace will start bawling and take to the streets in protest, while resources become increasingly scarce, animals disappear, the seasons turn upside down and the sea fills with plastic. We're never going to get anywhere like that. So the idea came to me to somehow make it so that people find their trough so disgusting that they end up turning away from it or tipping it over with their snout. Because truly, it really is disgusting, it's just that nobody wants to see it because it's far too inconvenient to have to change the way we live.'

To which Hildegarde, who in the meantime had made her way back towards us, added, 'We're going to wreak havoc, Blanche and I.'

He looked at the three of us, then he smiled.

'The giantess, the little fury and the girl with the broken body . . I like you. All three of you. Pierre de Rigny died fifty years ago, when he met Mother and received the *Darshan* for his birthday. The elders here will provide you with my death certificate. And as for our common ancestor, Auguste, it made me very happy, hearing everything you had to say about him. It could well be that he met his end in a way not dissimilar to my own approaching demise: surrounded by trees.'

'You won't leave everything to Auroville, then?'

'Certainly not! I care too much about this place to spoil it with that money.'

And then he did what my father always used to do when he wanted to let me know the conversation was over. He went back to what he was doing and we no longer existed. Voilà . . . voilà . . .

On the way back, Hildegarde and I didn't say a word to each other, and then, at some point, when we had pulled into a petrol station to fill up our mopeds, I broke the silence.

'Did you think about what would have happened if he hadn't left us the money?'

'Of course I thought about it . . .'

'Me too.'

'But it didn't come to that, so chill.'

Versailles
20 April 1871

Naked but for an oversized jacket and trousers which he was clinging onto so they did not fall down to his ankles, Auguste stood in silence before the desk of Monsieur, the Chief Executive of the Republic, Adolphe Thiers.

Cinched into his grey frock coat, every now and again Thiers would throw the young man a stony look as he signed the orders in the file of documents awaiting signature while an unobtrusive secretary turned the pages.

'You have your aunt to thank – a good and dear friend – for had it been left to me, I would have had you executed.'

Silence.

'Have you nothing to say?'

Auguste stared at his feet, which were black with grime. His head was spinning and he could muster only one thought, namely to curl up in a ball on the ground and sleep.

'Well then, clearly you do not have anything to say! That much is evident.'

Silence.

Thiers signed a few more documents, then dismissed the secretary with an abrupt gesture.

'I knew your grandfather very well, you know ... A fine friend ... Your brother Ferdinand bears such a resemblance to him ... He would have been proud ... I have not had any children, myself ...'

He sighed.

'He would have been proud. Indeed.'

The floor looked so appealing. He could perhaps have feigned a fainting fit. There was even a thick woollen rug. That way the midget could continue his lecturing in that sour voice of his. Yes, he would listen, but stretched out on that comfortable floor, not one rat in sight.

'Maintain one's rank … Does it mean anything to you, this expression? It doesn't, does it! Deplorable!'

On 2 April, galvanised into action by the progeny fate had delivered him, he had left with his Communard friends for the assault on Versailles, but having little experience in military matters, and confronted by a professional army, the troops had been rapidly encircled and taken prisoner. He had witnessed the summary execution of his leader, Duval, as well as numerous fellow Communards, especially those white-haired comrades who had been forced by their adversaries to break rank and were then shot on suspicion of being Forty-Eighters. He had then been paraded with the survivors through the streets of Versailles to the boos of the population. He had been spat upon, women had scratched him in the face and he had been struck with an umbrella until it broke on his back, then he had been made to kneel before each church in the town, like so many Stations of the Cross, in order to beg God's forgiveness. He had even had his trousers torn off, and thus he found himself half-naked when he was thrown into one of those Versailles dungeons used over the centuries by the kings of France to rid themselves of their political opponents. He had been rotting there ever since.

Thiers was still observing him as he continued absentmindedly to reconfigure the objects on his desk.

'Where I managed to achieve nothing with those damnable Prussians, you Communards have worked miracles. Can you believe they are returning all our soldiers to us and even permitting us to increase the contingent allowed in our peace accords. Bismarck has gone so far as to enjoin us to raise the finest army we have ever had – and I use his words – to allow us to crush you, that is how much you disgust him. Ah yes, you have even succeeded in repelling the Prussians ... Now that is saying something indeed!'

Silence.

'Where was it you were heading with your battalion of drunkards disguised as soldiers? Were you wanting to invade Versailles, is that it?'

He struck the table with his fist.

'Is that it?'

'*Vive la Commune!*' said Auguste in so feeble a voice it seemed to emerge from the bottom of a well.

Thiers murmured, 'What am I to do with you, de Rigny? Be off, disappear, you reek of dead animal.'

At the end of the Bloody Week, his cellmates were shot, if they had not already died from their wounds or from their time in prison. For a few months he, along with others, shared the fate of Théophile Ferré, the man who alongside the anarchist Pindy had ordered the destruction of all Paris's civil records. Upon learning this, Auguste had burst into sobs, for reasons that were not truly understood by the person communicating the news. Every man in his cell was condemned to death and executed, one after the other, through to the month of December. Auguste, however, was sentenced to deportation to New Caledonia, because his role in the Commune was found to be of minor importance, but at the trial rumour already had it that he would be off-loaded somewhere en route, and at some other French port moreover. It wasn't yet known precisely where ... Senegal, Madagascar, Mauritius ... it would depend on the route taken, but regardless the matter had in principle been agreed.

A place where conditions were mild and where he would be safe.

In that regard, Aunt Clothilde had been most insistent with her old friend.

Acknowledgements

The idea for my book followed my reading of Thomas Piketty's treatise *Le capital au XXIe siècle* (*Capital in the Twenty-First Century*), a work that I found rigorous and unbiased, and which helped me understand the origins of this vague intuition I had that our twenty-first-century society bore an increasing resemblance to that of the nineteenth century.

The historical events my characters describe and comment on stem from a mixture of my readings, articles that appeared in newspapers from the time, from my imagination, but most of all from my ignorance.

A special mention to Paul Lidsky's extraordinary work *Les écrivains contre la Commune*. Borrow it, read it – it is fabulous! And also, huge thanks to Les Amis de la Commune de Paris, and in particular to John Sutton, who guided my readings.

As for what truly is the bible on the subject of military substitution, see: Bernard Schnapper's *Le remplacement militaire en France: Quelques aspects politiques, économiques et sociaux du recrutement au XIXe siècle*. See also the newspaper *L'Assurance*, writing on the reform of military substitution from 1868 to the declaration of war against Prussia.

As for Philippe de Rigny's hijinks and meroxage

attempts on the high seas, I am entirely indebted to the work of Bernard Dussol and Charlotte Nithart – *Le Cargo de la honte; l'effroyable odyssée du Probo Koala*, from which it is evident that truth is stranger than fiction and that writers play it safe when it comes to portraying rapacity. Read it and be outraged.

Special thanks to the Association Robin des Bois for their work tracing the floating hulks that continue to transport pollutants on the high seas.

For political commentary on the subject of contemporary art and popular education, Franck Lepage's clear-sighted dramatised lectures were hugely inspiring. They can be found on YouTube.

See also Peter Watkins' five-and-a-half-hour film *La Commune (Paris, 1871)* and Gérard Mordillat's *La Forteresse assiégée* with commentary by Frédéric Gros – among others – author of the book, *Désobéir (Disobey)*, which also served as inspiration.

Thanks also to my ever-reliable proofreaders, Antony and Jean, who, with their patient word-for-word reading, allow me to forget that I was granted special time dispensation for my baccalaureat … And to my agent, Danièle D'Antoni, who would like to change the world through strict application of the law and whose dream inspired the end of this novel.

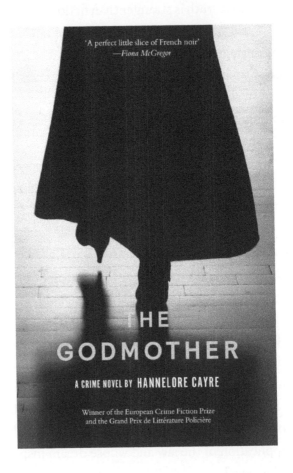

'A perfect little slice of French noir'
—Fiona McGregor

THE
GODMOTHER

A CRIME NOVEL BY HANNELORE CAYRE

Winner of the European Crime Fiction Prize
and the Grand Prix de Littérature Policière

Book club notes available from
blackincbooks.com.au

Lightning Source UK Ltd.
Milton Keynes UK
UKHW011843171221
395826UK00001B/204